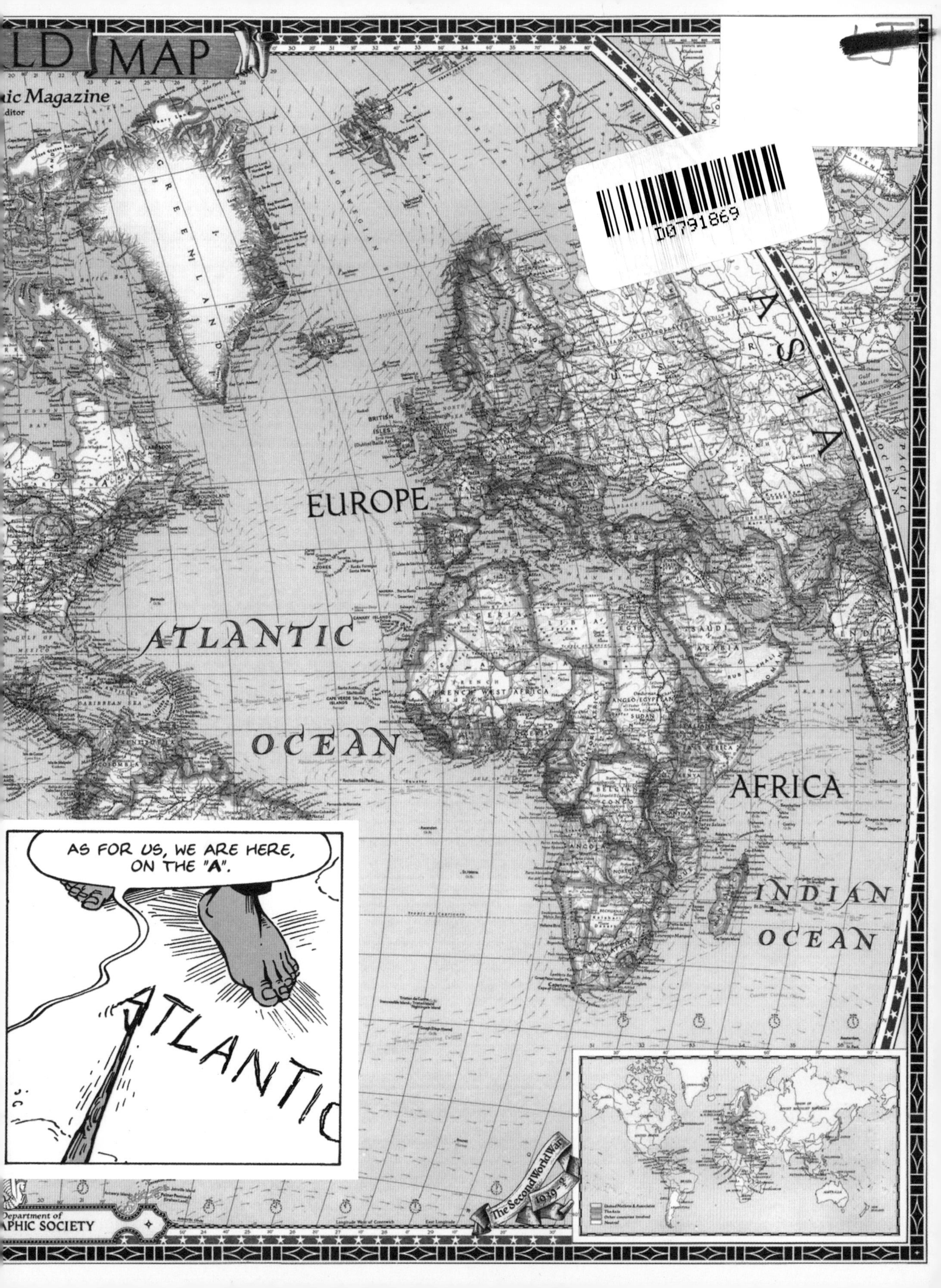
MAP
EUROPE
ASIA
ATLANTIC
OCEAN
AFRICA
INDIAN
OCEAN
AS FOR US, WE ARE HERE, ON THE "A".
The Second World War

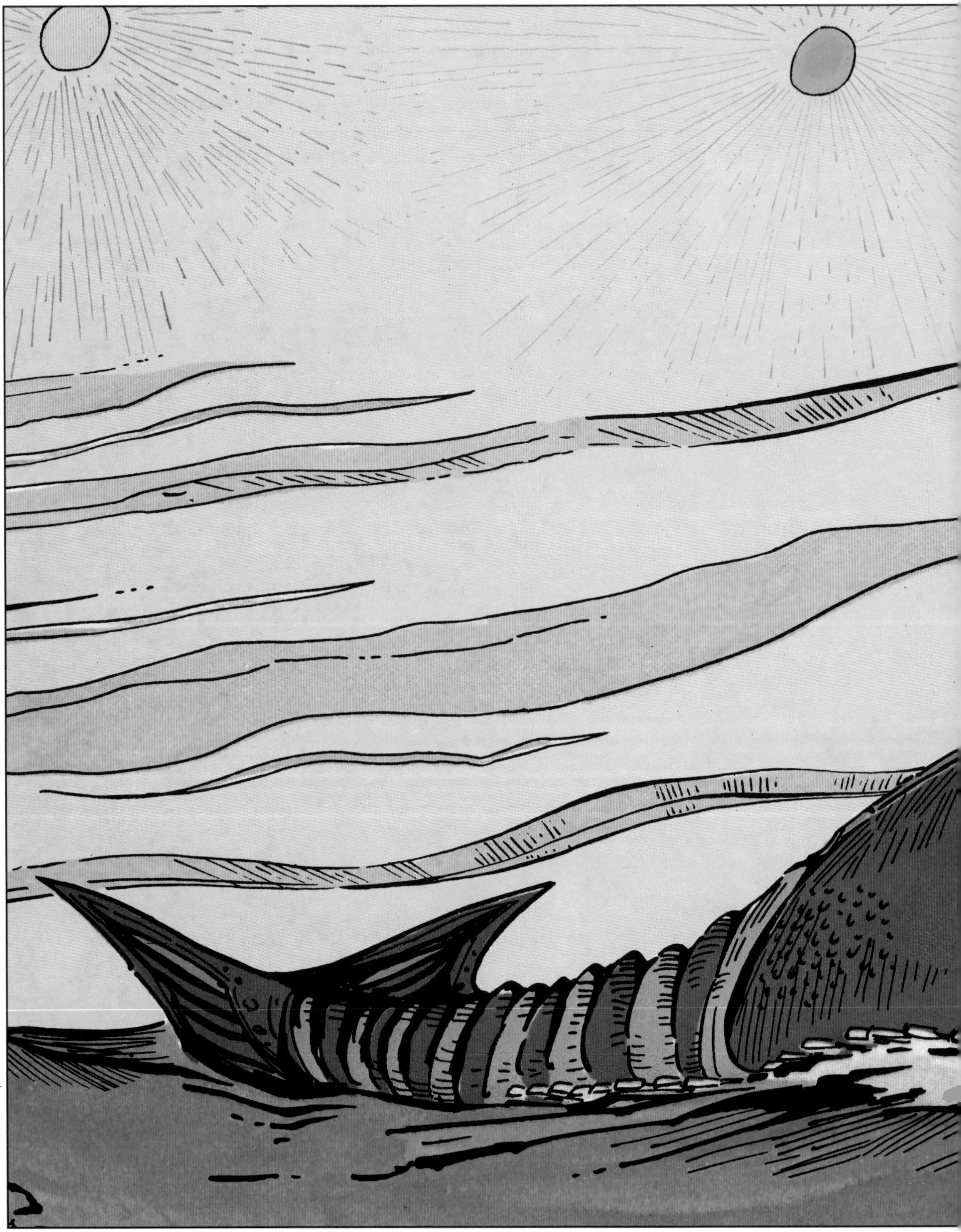

FRED

THE SUSPENDED CASTLE

A PHILEMON ADVENTURE

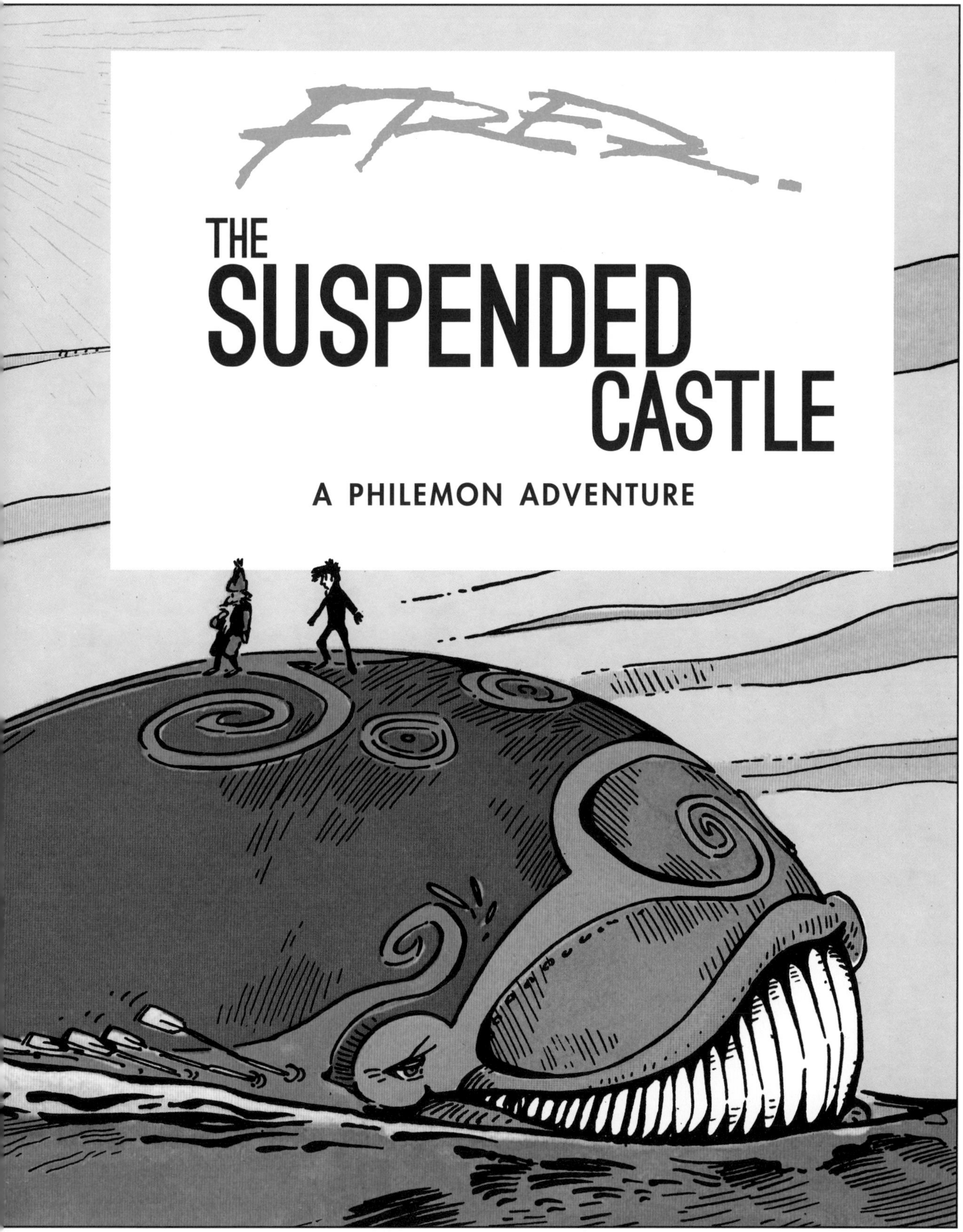

Editorial Director: F R A N Ç O I S E   M O U L Y

Managing Editor: S A S H A   S T E I N B E R G

Book Design: F R A N Ç O I S E   M O U L Y

Hand-lettering: M Y K E N   B O M B E R G E R   &   F R E D

F R E D ' S artwork was drawn in India ink, watercolor, and gouache.

FOR VISUAL READERS
TOON
GRAPHICS

A TOON Graphic™ © 2015 TOON Books, an imprint of RAW Junior, LLC, 27 Greene Street, New York, NY 10013. Original text and illustrations from *Philémon et le château suspendu*, © 1973 DARGAUD. Translation, ancillary material, and TOON Graphic™ adaptation © 2015 RAW Junior, LLC. No part of this book may be used or reproduced in any manner whatsoever without written permission except in the case of brief quotations embodied in critical articles and reviews. TOON Graphics™, TOON Books®, LITTLE LIT® and TOON Into Reading!™ are trademarks of RAW Junior, LLC. All rights reserved. All our books are Smyth Sewn (the highest library-quality binding available) and printed with soy-based inks on acid-free, woodfree paper harvested from responsible sources. Printed in China by C&C Offset Printing Co., Ltd. Distributed to the trade by Consortium Book Sales and Distribution, Inc.; orders (800) 283-3572 34; orderentry@perseusbooks.com; www.cbsd.com.
Library of Congress Cataloging-in-Publication Data available upon request.

ISBN 978-1-935179-86-3 (hardcover)

15 16 17 18 19 20 C&C 10 9 8 7 6 5 4 3 2 1

W W W . T O O N - B O O K S . C O M

THE SUSPENDED CASTLE

A PHILEMON ADVENTURE

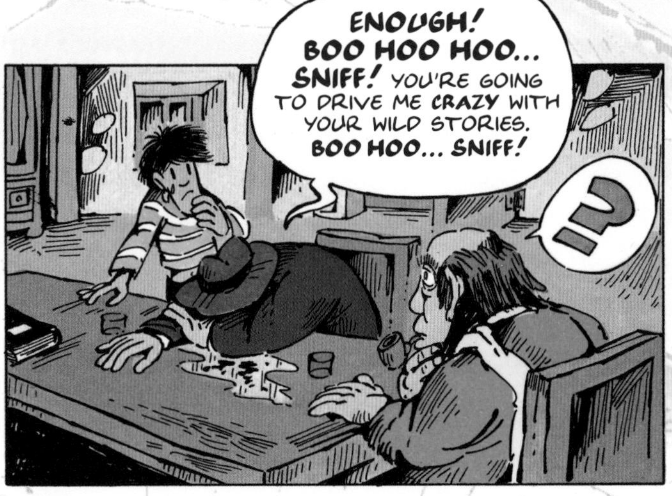
ENOUGH! BOO HOO HOO... SNIFF! YOU'RE GOING TO DRIVE ME CRAZY WITH YOUR WILD STORIES. BOO HOO... SNIFF!
!?

A TOON GRAPHIC BY

FRED

Translated by RICHARD KUTNER

MEET PHILEMON

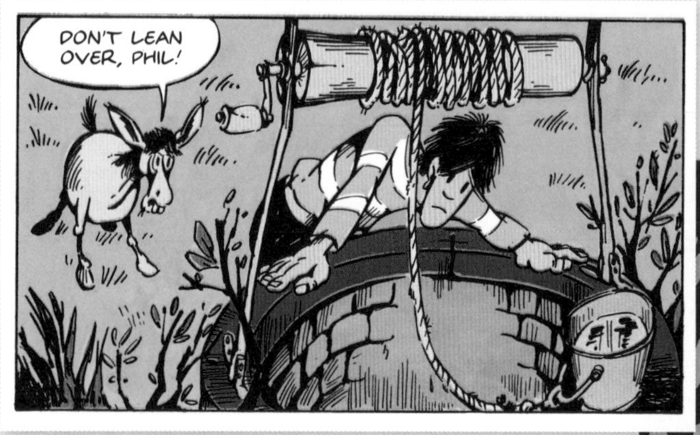
DON'T LEAN OVER, PHIL!

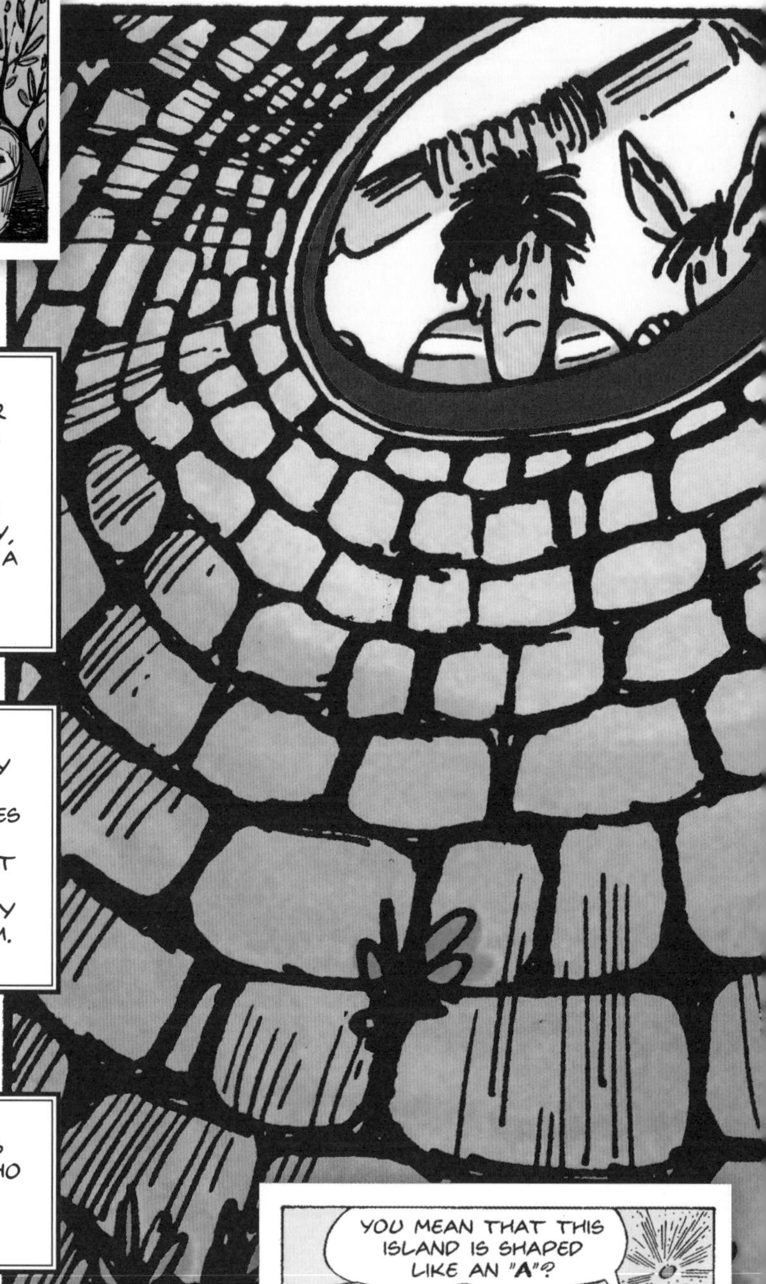

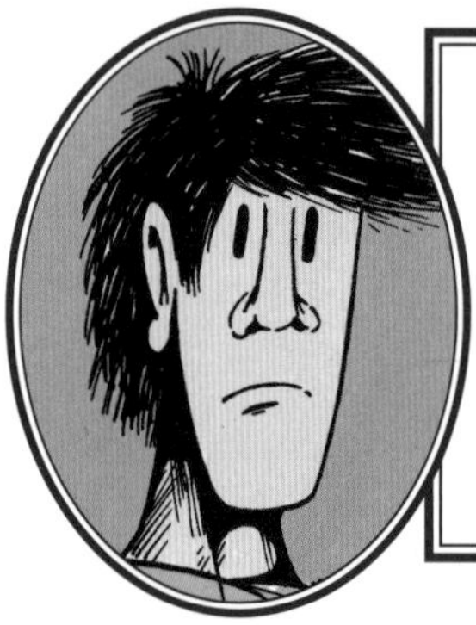

PHILEMON IS AN IMAGINATIVE TEENAGER WHO LIVES ON A FARM IN FRANCE, BACK IN THE 1960S. WHEN A MESSAGE IN A BOTTLE SPARKS HIS CURIOSITY, HE FALLS RIGHT INTO A WORLD OF FANTASTIC ADVENTURES...

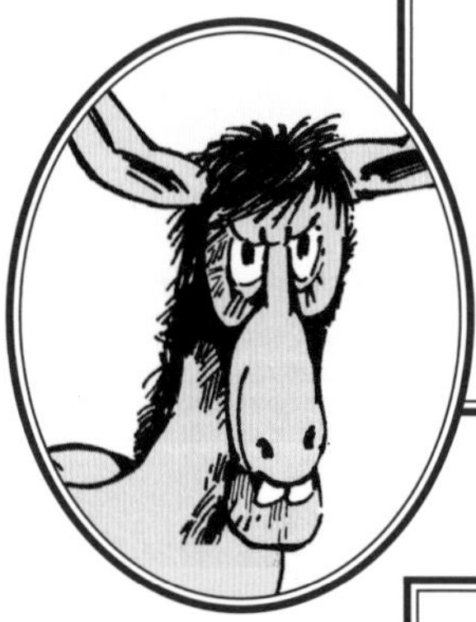

ANATOLE IS A DONKEY AND PHIL'S TRUSTY FRIEND. ANATOLE TRIES TO HELP PHIL STAY OUT OF TROUBLE, BUT PHIL'S ADVENTUROUS SPIRIT AND CURIOSITY GET THE BEST OF HIM.

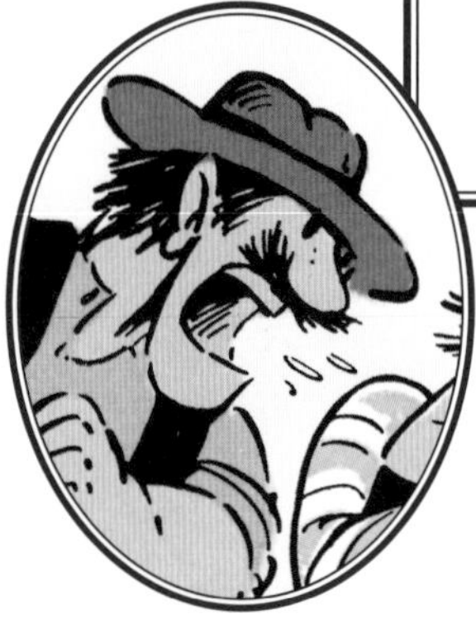

HECTOR IS PHILEMON'S GROUCHY FATHER, WHO REFUSES TO BELIEVE PHIL'S WILD STORIES.

PHILEMON FALLS DOWN A WELL AND WAKES UP ON A STRANGE ISLAND IN THE MIDDLE OF THE ATLANTIC. THERE HE MEETS A WELL DIGGER, **MR. BARTHOLOMEW**, WHO LANDED THERE YEARS AGO. UNFORTUNATELY, THE TWO NEW FRIENDS ARE SEPARATED.

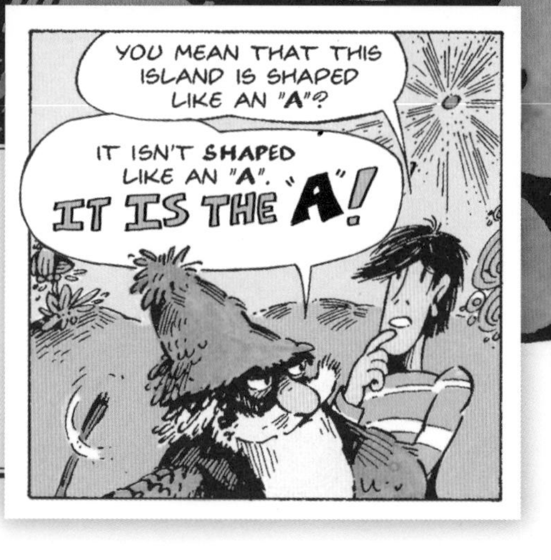
YOU MEAN THAT THIS ISLAND IS SHAPED LIKE AN "A"?
IT ISN'T SHAPED LIKE AN "A". IT IS THE A!

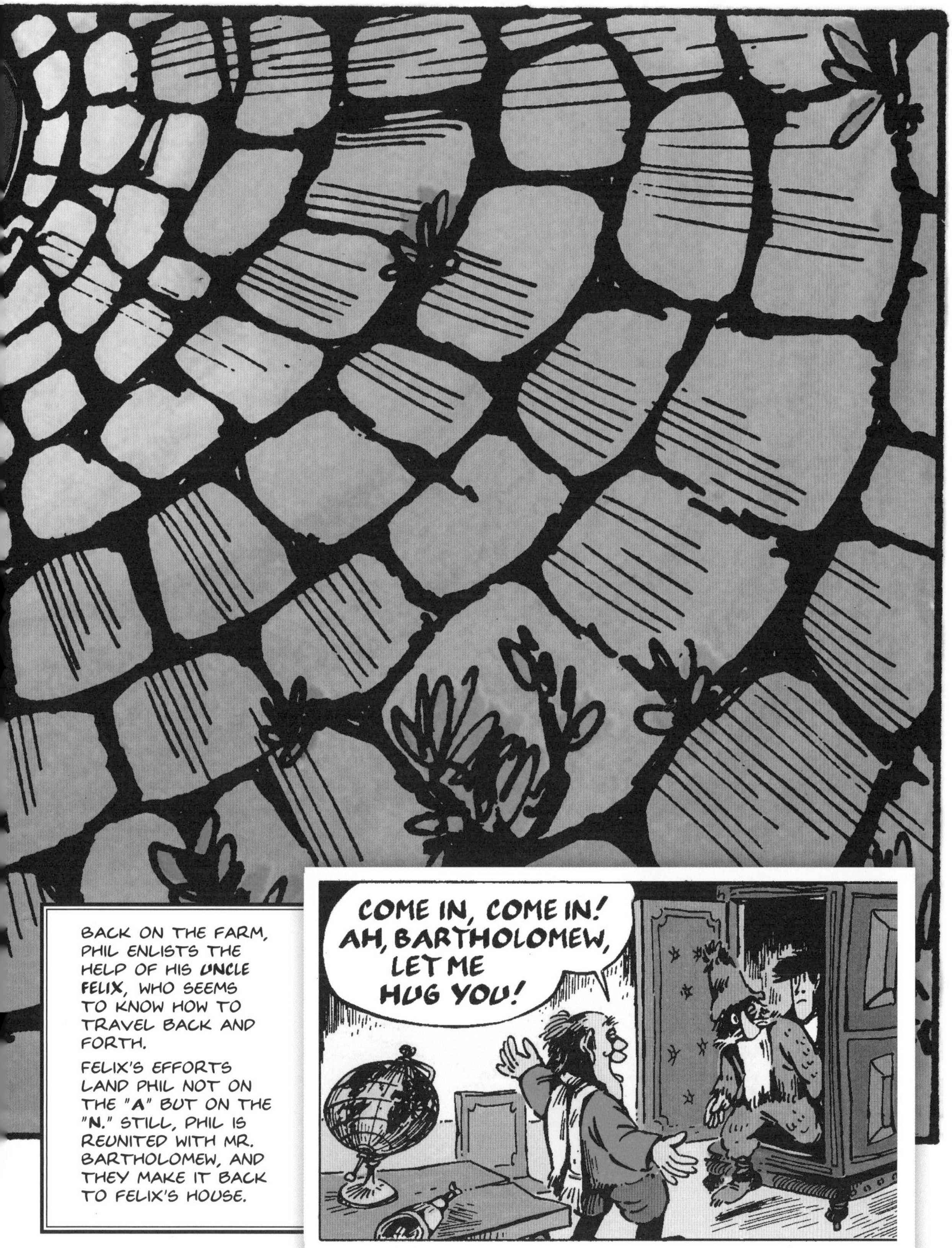
BACK ON THE FARM, PHIL ENLISTS THE HELP OF HIS UNCLE FELIX, WHO SEEMS TO KNOW HOW TO TRAVEL BACK AND FORTH.
FELIX'S EFFORTS LAND PHIL NOT ON THE "A" BUT ON THE "N." STILL, PHIL IS REUNITED WITH MR. BARTHOLOMEW, AND THEY MAKE IT BACK TO FELIX'S HOUSE.
COME IN, COME IN! AH, BARTHOLOMEW, LET ME HUG YOU!

THE PHILEMON ADVENTURES

CAST AWAY ON THE LETTER A

THE WILD PIANO

THE SUSPENDED CASTLE

THE IMPOSSIBLE VOYAGE

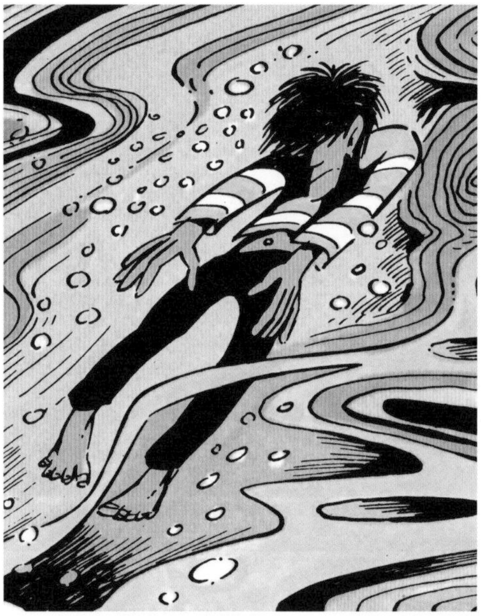

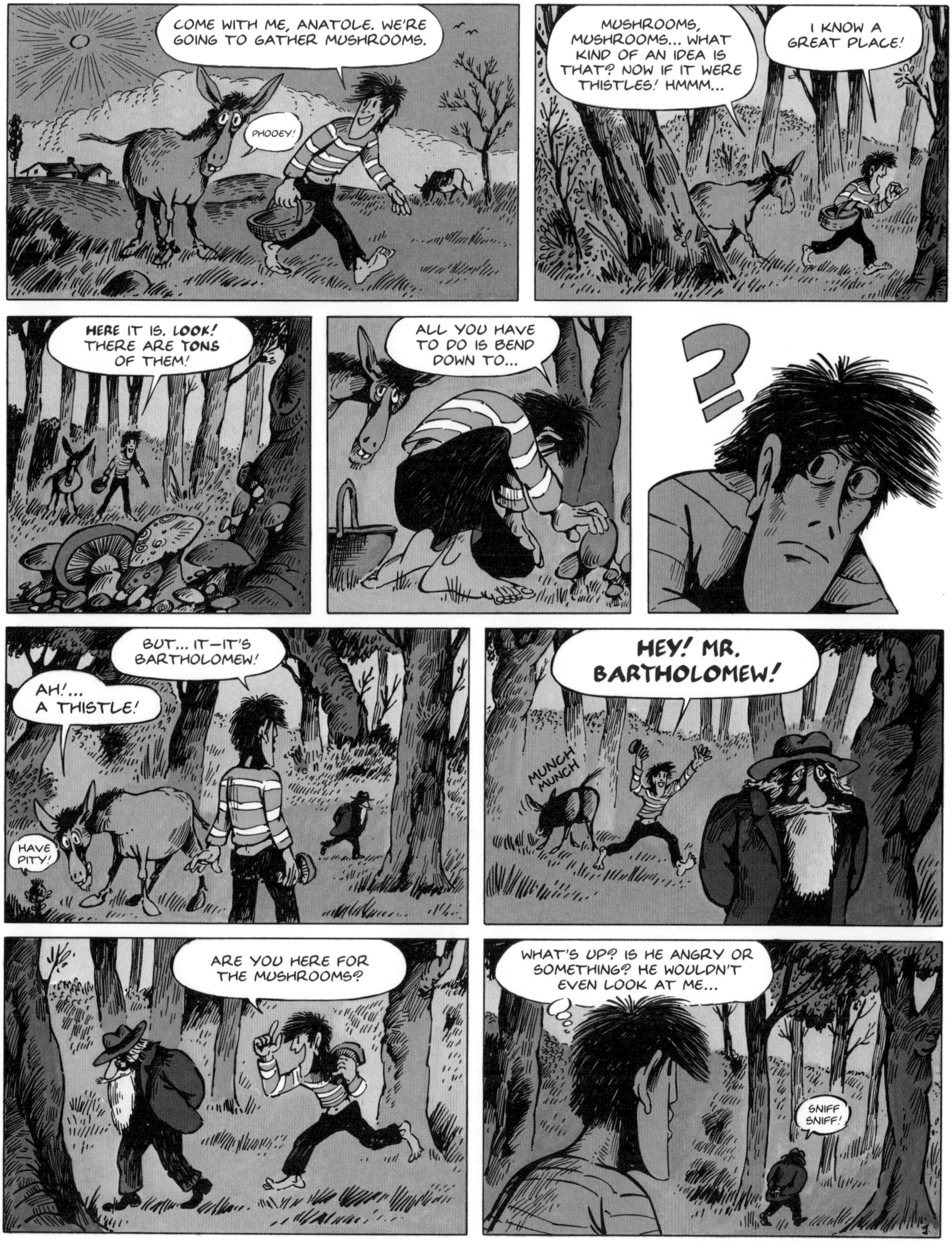
COME WITH ME, ANATOLE. WE'RE GOING TO GATHER MUSHROOMS.
PHOOEY!
MUSHROOMS, MUSHROOMS... WHAT KIND OF AN IDEA IS THAT? NOW IF IT WERE THISTLES! HMMM...
I KNOW A GREAT PLACE!
HERE IT IS. LOOK! THERE ARE TONS OF THEM!
ALL YOU HAVE TO DO IS BEND DOWN TO...
?
BUT... IT—IT'S BARTHOLOMEW!
AH!... A THISTLE!
HAVE PITY!
HEY! MR. BARTHOLOMEW!
MUNCH MUNCH
ARE YOU HERE FOR THE MUSHROOMS?
WHAT'S UP? IS HE ANGRY OR SOMETHING? HE WOULDN'T EVEN LOOK AT ME...
SNIFF SNIFF!

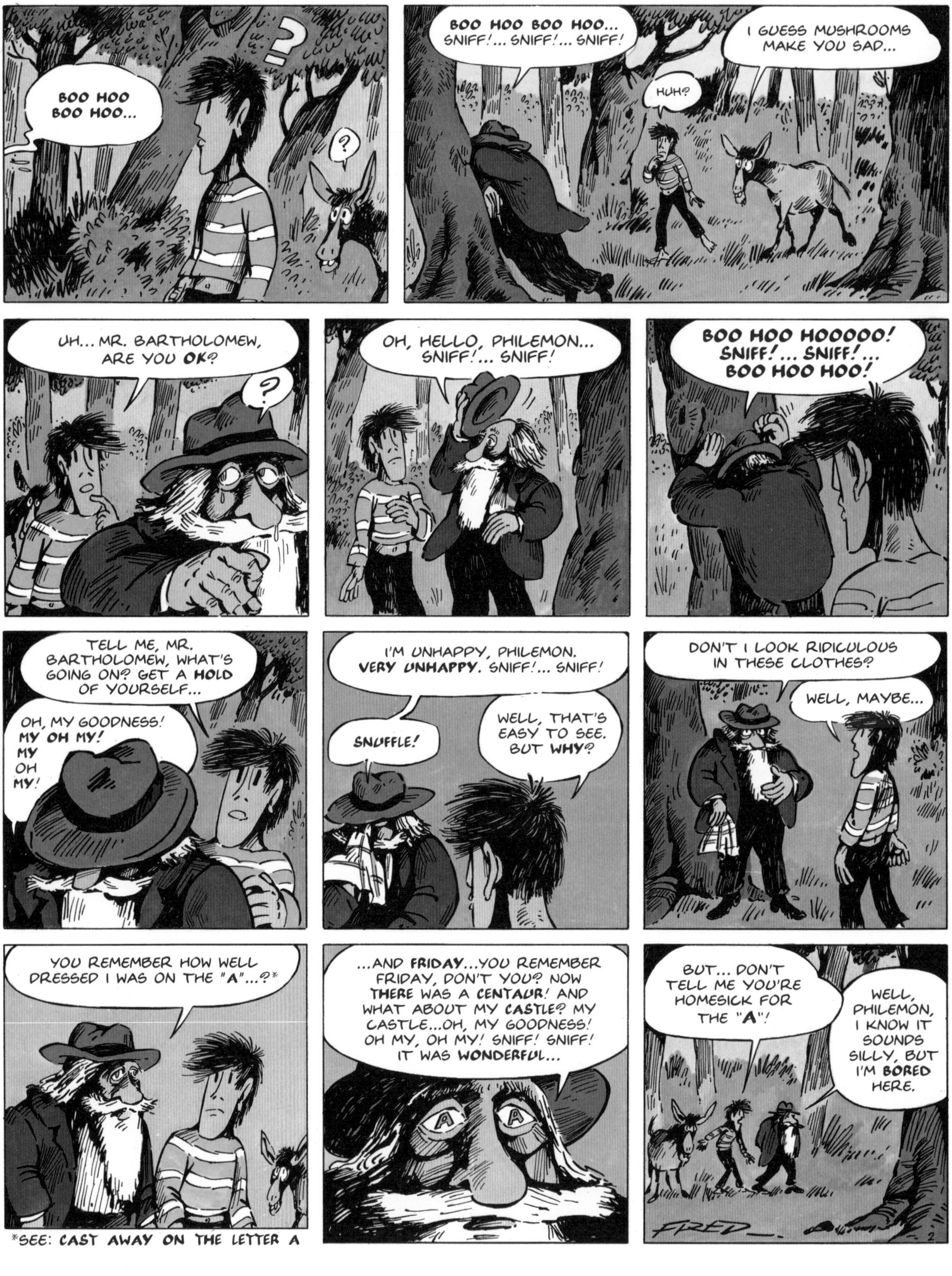

BOO HOO BOO HOO...
?
?
BOO HOO BOO HOO... SNIFF!... SNIFF!... SNIFF!
HUH?
I GUESS MUSHROOMS MAKE YOU SAD...
UH... MR. BARTHOLOMEW, ARE YOU OK?
?
OH, HELLO, PHILEMON... SNIFF!... SNIFF!
BOO HOO HOOOOO! SNIFF!... SNIFF!... BOO HOO HOO!
TELL ME, MR. BARTHOLOMEW, WHAT'S GOING ON? GET A HOLD OF YOURSELF...
OH, MY GOODNESS! MY OH MY! MY OH MY!
I'M UNHAPPY, PHILEMON. VERY UNHAPPY. SNIFF!... SNIFF!
SNUFFLE!
WELL, THAT'S EASY TO SEE. BUT WHY?
DON'T I LOOK RIDICULOUS IN THESE CLOTHES?
WELL, MAYBE...
YOU REMEMBER HOW WELL DRESSED I WAS ON THE "A"...?*
...AND FRIDAY...YOU REMEMBER FRIDAY, DON'T YOU? NOW THERE WAS A CENTAUR! AND WHAT ABOUT MY CASTLE? MY CASTLE...OH, MY GOODNESS! OH MY, OH MY! SNIFF! SNIFF! IT WAS WONDERFUL...
BUT... DON'T TELL ME YOU'RE HOMESICK FOR THE "A"!
WELL, PHILEMON, I KNOW IT SOUNDS SILLY, BUT I'M BORED HERE.
FRED
2

*SEE: CAST AWAY ON THE LETTER A

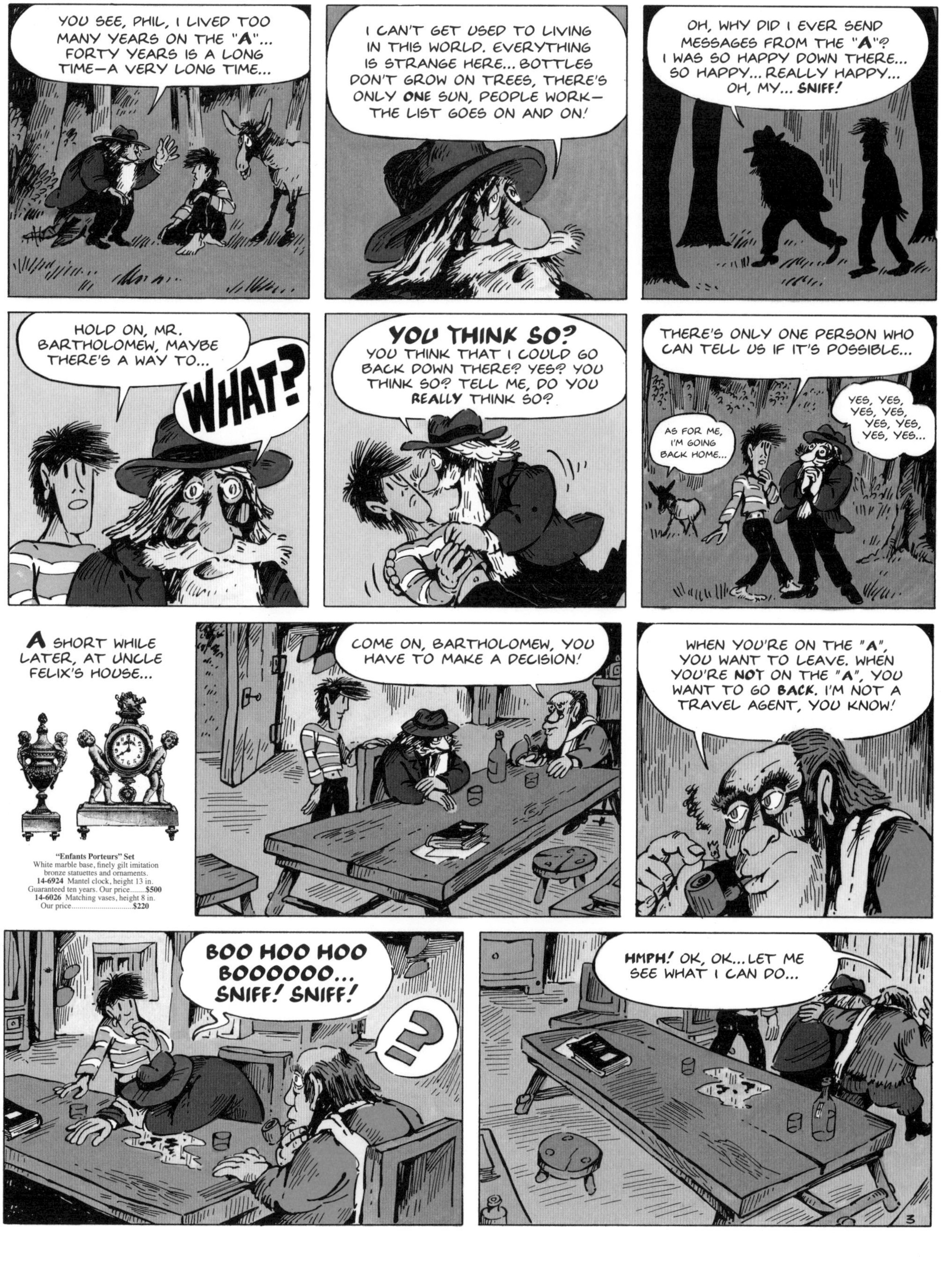
YOU SEE, PHIL, I LIVED TOO MANY YEARS ON THE "A"... FORTY YEARS IS A LONG TIME—A VERY LONG TIME...
I CAN'T GET USED TO LIVING IN THIS WORLD. EVERYTHING IS STRANGE HERE... BOTTLES DON'T GROW ON TREES, THERE'S ONLY ONE SUN, PEOPLE WORK—THE LIST GOES ON AND ON!
OH, WHY DID I EVER SEND MESSAGES FROM THE "A"? I WAS SO HAPPY DOWN THERE... SO HAPPY... REALLY HAPPY... OH, MY... SNIFF!
HOLD ON, MR. BARTHOLOMEW, MAYBE THERE'S A WAY TO...
WHAT?
YOU THINK SO? YOU THINK THAT I COULD GO BACK DOWN THERE? YES? YOU THINK SO? TELL ME, DO YOU REALLY THINK SO?
THERE'S ONLY ONE PERSON WHO CAN TELL US IF IT'S POSSIBLE...
AS FOR ME, I'M GOING BACK HOME...
YES, YES, YES, YES, YES, YES, YES, YES...
A SHORT WHILE LATER, AT UNCLE FELIX'S HOUSE...
"Enfants Porteurs" Set
White marble base, finely gilt imitation bronze statuettes and ornaments.
14-6924 Mantel clock, height 13 in. Guaranteed ten years. Our price........$500
14-6026 Matching vases, height 8 in. Our price..............................$220
COME ON, BARTHOLOMEW, YOU HAVE TO MAKE A DECISION!
WHEN YOU'RE ON THE "A", YOU WANT TO LEAVE. WHEN YOU'RE NOT ON THE "A", YOU WANT TO GO BACK. I'M NOT A TRAVEL AGENT, YOU KNOW!
BOO HOO HOO BOOOOOO... SNIFF! SNIFF!
?
HMPH! OK, OK... LET ME SEE WHAT I CAN DO...
3

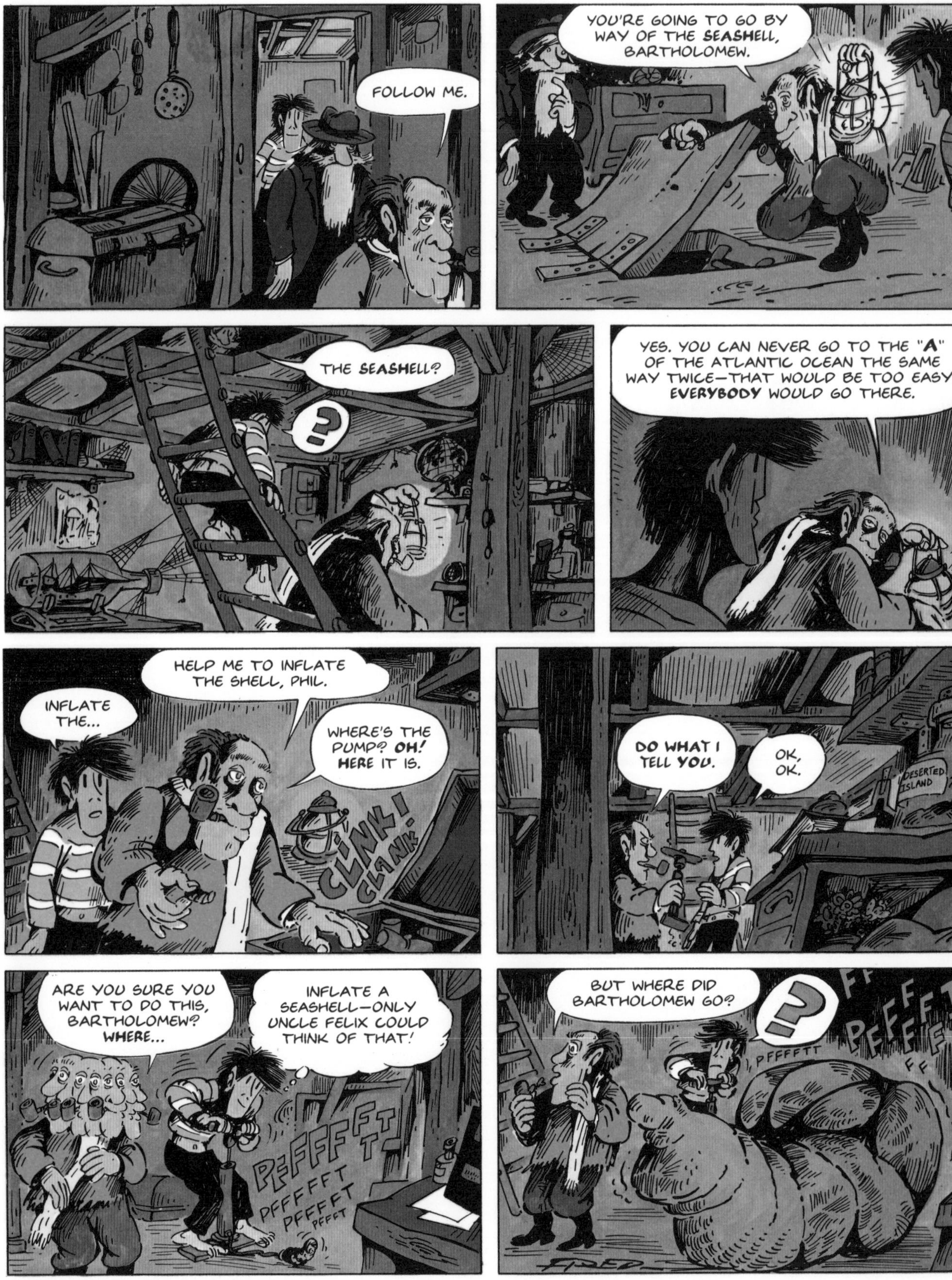
FOLLOW ME.
YOU'RE GOING TO GO BY WAY OF THE SEASHELL, BARTHOLOMEW.
THE SEASHELL?
?
YES. YOU CAN NEVER GO TO THE "A" OF THE ATLANTIC OCEAN THE SAME WAY TWICE—THAT WOULD BE TOO EASY! EVERYBODY WOULD GO THERE.
HELP ME TO INFLATE THE SHELL, PHIL.
INFLATE THE...
WHERE'S THE PUMP? OH! HERE IT IS.
CLINK! CLANK
DO WHAT I TELL YOU.
OK, OK.
DESERTED ISLAND
ARE YOU SURE YOU WANT TO DO THIS, BARTHOLOMEW? WHERE...
INFLATE A SEASHELL—ONLY UNCLE FELIX COULD THINK OF THAT!
PFFFFFTT
PFFFFFT
PFFFFFT
PFFFT
BUT WHERE DID BARTHOLOMEW GO?
?
PFFFFFTT
PFFFFTT

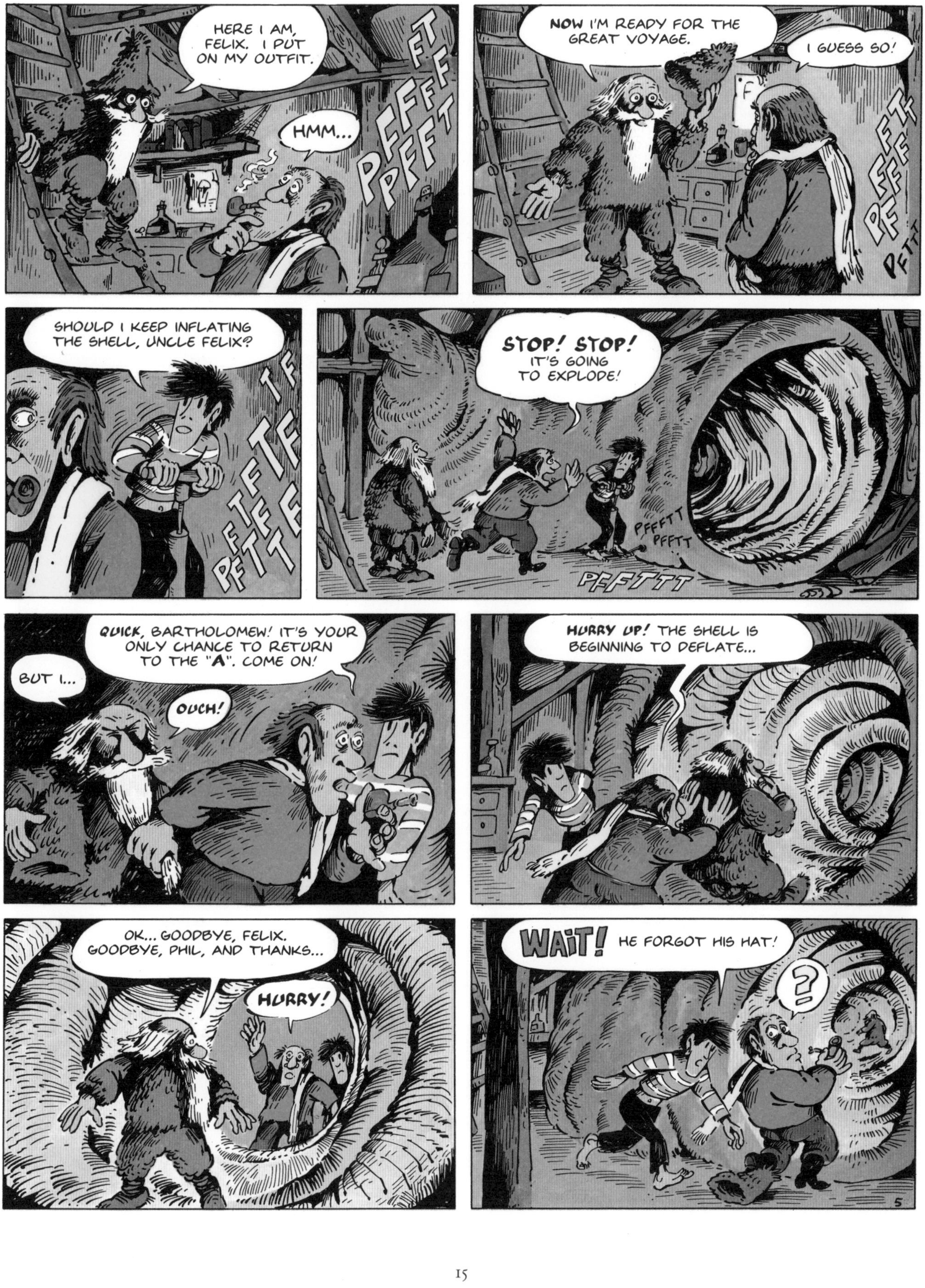
HERE I AM, FELIX. I PUT ON MY OUTFIT.
HMM...
FT PFFFFT PFFFT
NOW I'M READY FOR THE GREAT VOYAGE.
I GUESS SO!
PFFFT PFFT
SHOULD I KEEP INFLATING THE SHELL, UNCLE FELIX?
TF PFTFT PFTFT
STOP! STOP! IT'S GOING TO EXPLODE!
PFFFTT PFFTT
PFFTTT
QUICK, BARTHOLOMEW! IT'S YOUR ONLY CHANCE TO RETURN TO THE "A". COME ON!
BUT I...
OUCH!
HURRY UP! THE SHELL IS BEGINNING TO DEFLATE...
OK... GOODBYE, FELIX. GOODBYE, PHIL, AND THANKS...
HURRY!
WAIT! HE FORGOT HIS HAT!
?
5

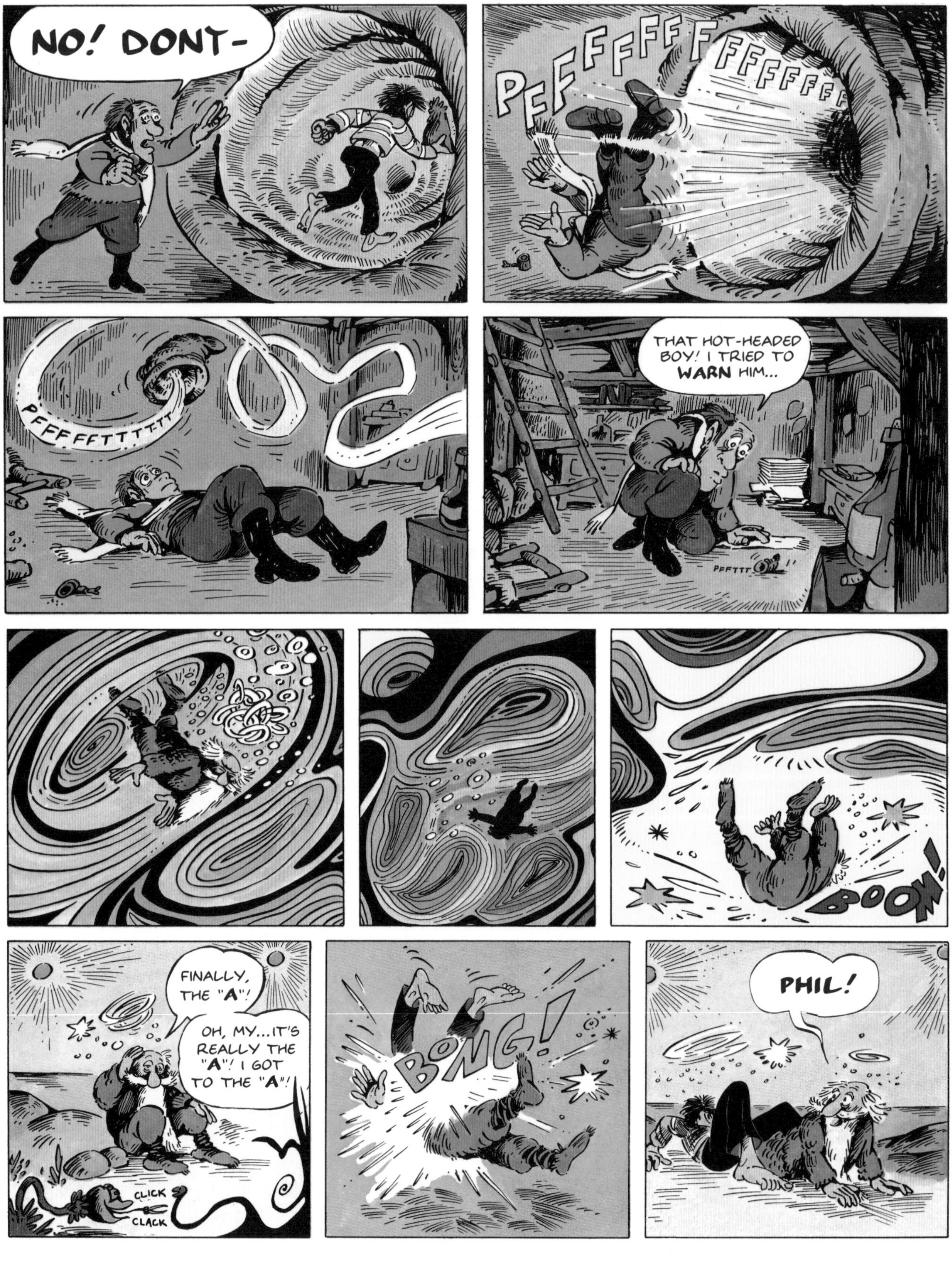
NO! DONT-
PFFFFFFFFFFFFFFF
PFFFFFTTTTTTT
THAT HOT-HEADED BOY! I TRIED TO **WARN** HIM...
PFFTTT
BOOM!
FINALLY, THE "A"!
OH, MY...IT'S REALLY THE "A"! I GOT TO THE "A"!
CLICK
CLACK
BONG!
PHIL!

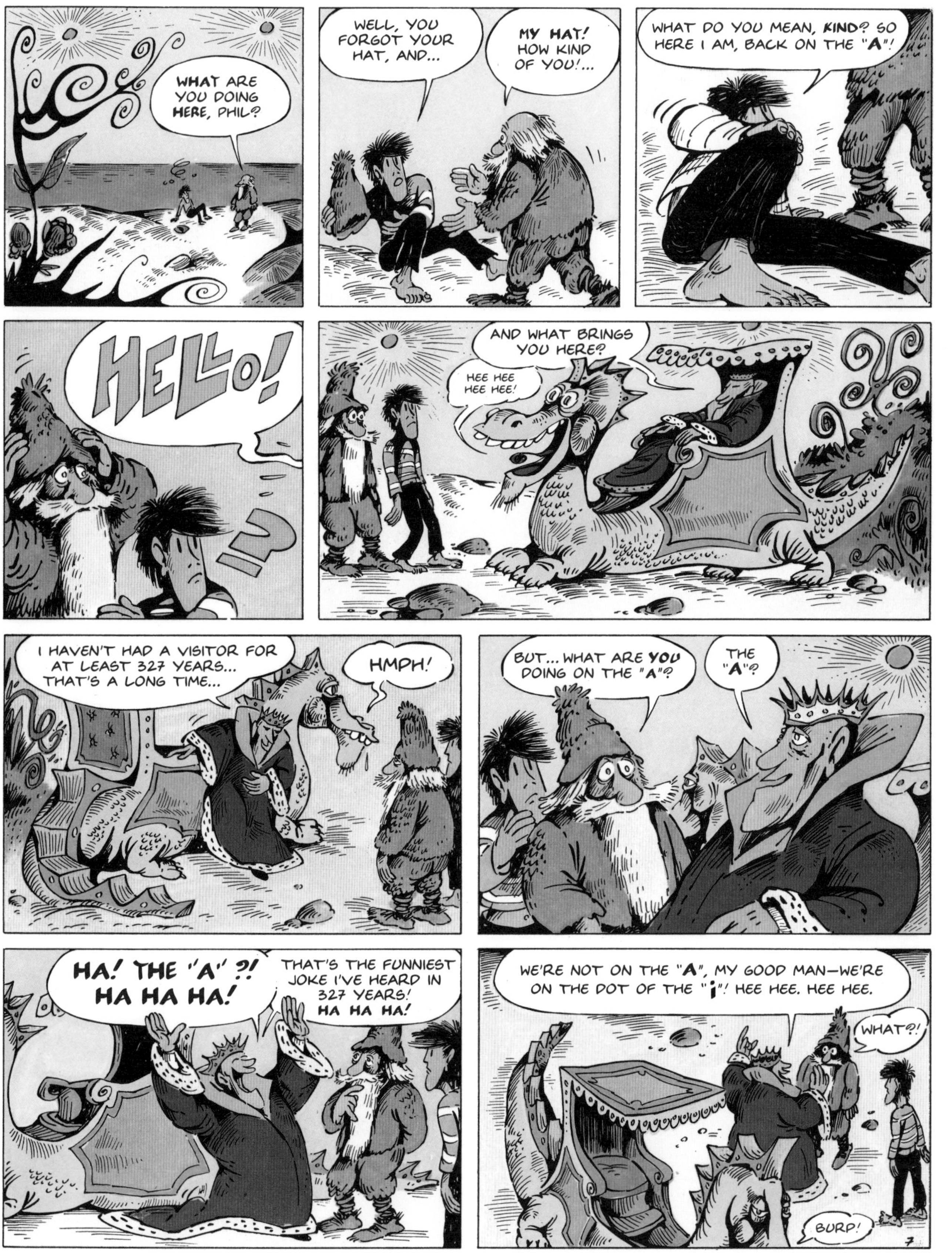
WHAT ARE YOU DOING HERE, PHIL?
WELL, YOU FORGOT YOUR HAT, AND...
MY HAT! HOW KIND OF YOU!...
WHAT DO YOU MEAN, KIND? SO HERE I AM, BACK ON THE "A"!
HELLO!
?
AND WHAT BRINGS YOU HERE?
HEE HEE HEE HEE!
I HAVEN'T HAD A VISITOR FOR AT LEAST 327 YEARS... THAT'S A LONG TIME...
HMPH!
BUT... WHAT ARE YOU DOING ON THE "A"?
THE "A"?
HA! THE "A" ?! HA HA HA!
THAT'S THE FUNNIEST JOKE I'VE HEARD IN 327 YEARS! HA HA HA!
WE'RE NOT ON THE "A", MY GOOD MAN—WE'RE ON THE DOT OF THE "i"! HEE HEE. HEE HEE.
WHAT?!
BURP!
7

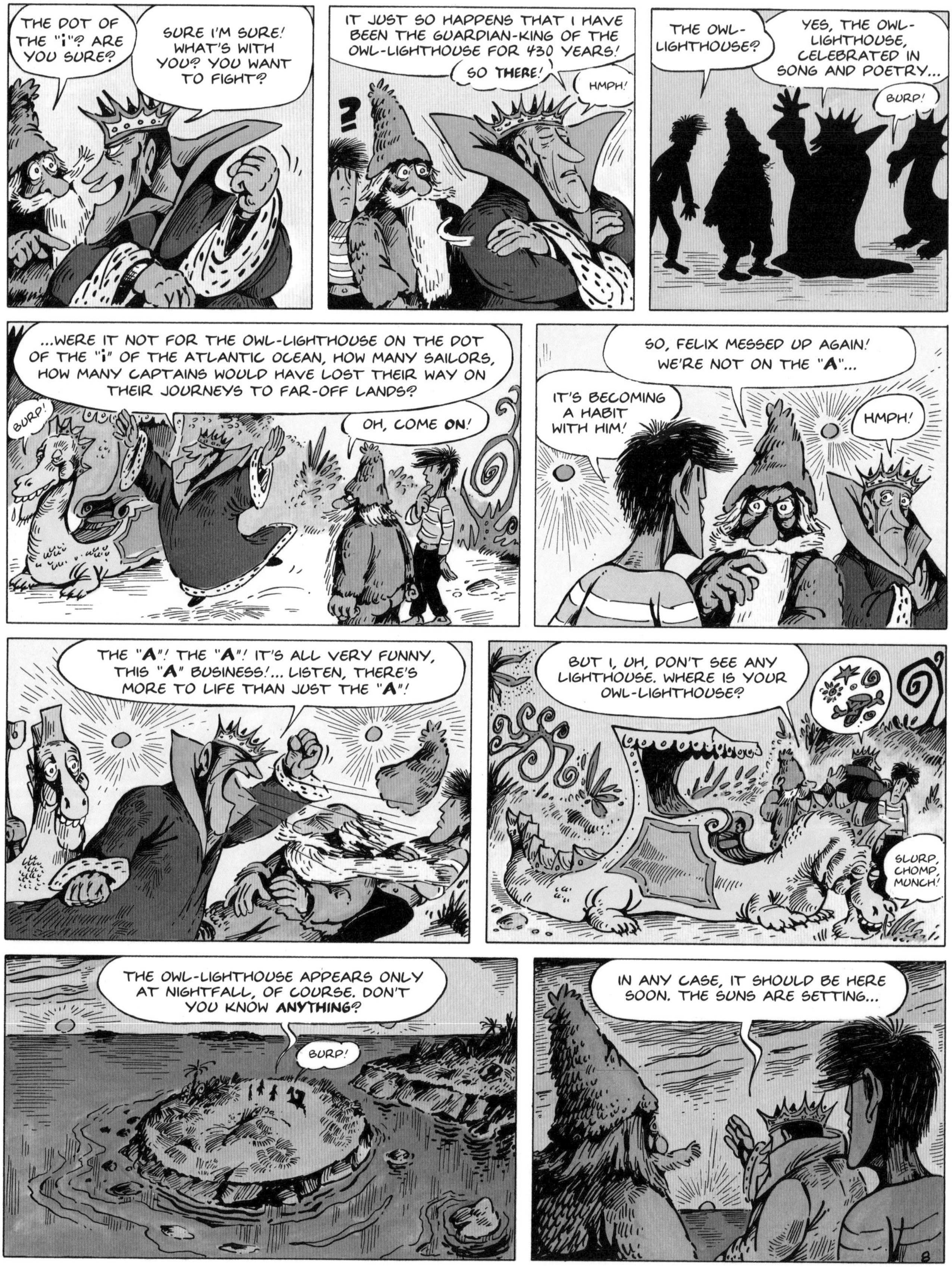
THE DOT OF THE "i"? ARE YOU SURE?
SURE I'M SURE! WHAT'S WITH YOU? YOU WANT TO FIGHT?
IT JUST SO HAPPENS THAT I HAVE BEEN THE GUARDIAN-KING OF THE OWL-LIGHTHOUSE FOR 430 YEARS!
SO THERE!
HMPH!
?
THE OWL-LIGHTHOUSE?
YES, THE OWL-LIGHTHOUSE, CELEBRATED IN SONG AND POETRY...
BURP!
...WERE IT NOT FOR THE OWL-LIGHTHOUSE ON THE DOT OF THE "i" OF THE ATLANTIC OCEAN, HOW MANY SAILORS, HOW MANY CAPTAINS WOULD HAVE LOST THEIR WAY ON THEIR JOURNEYS TO FAR-OFF LANDS?
BURP!
OH, COME ON!
SO, FELIX MESSED UP AGAIN! WE'RE NOT ON THE "A"...
IT'S BECOMING A HABIT WITH HIM!
HMPH!
THE "A"! THE "A"! IT'S ALL VERY FUNNY, THIS "A" BUSINESS!... LISTEN, THERE'S MORE TO LIFE THAN JUST THE "A"!
BUT I, UH, DON'T SEE ANY LIGHTHOUSE. WHERE IS YOUR OWL-LIGHTHOUSE?
SLURP, CHOMP, MUNCH!
THE OWL-LIGHTHOUSE APPEARS ONLY AT NIGHTFALL, OF COURSE. DON'T YOU KNOW ANYTHING?
BURP!
IN ANY CASE, IT SHOULD BE HERE SOON. THE SUNS ARE SETTING...
8

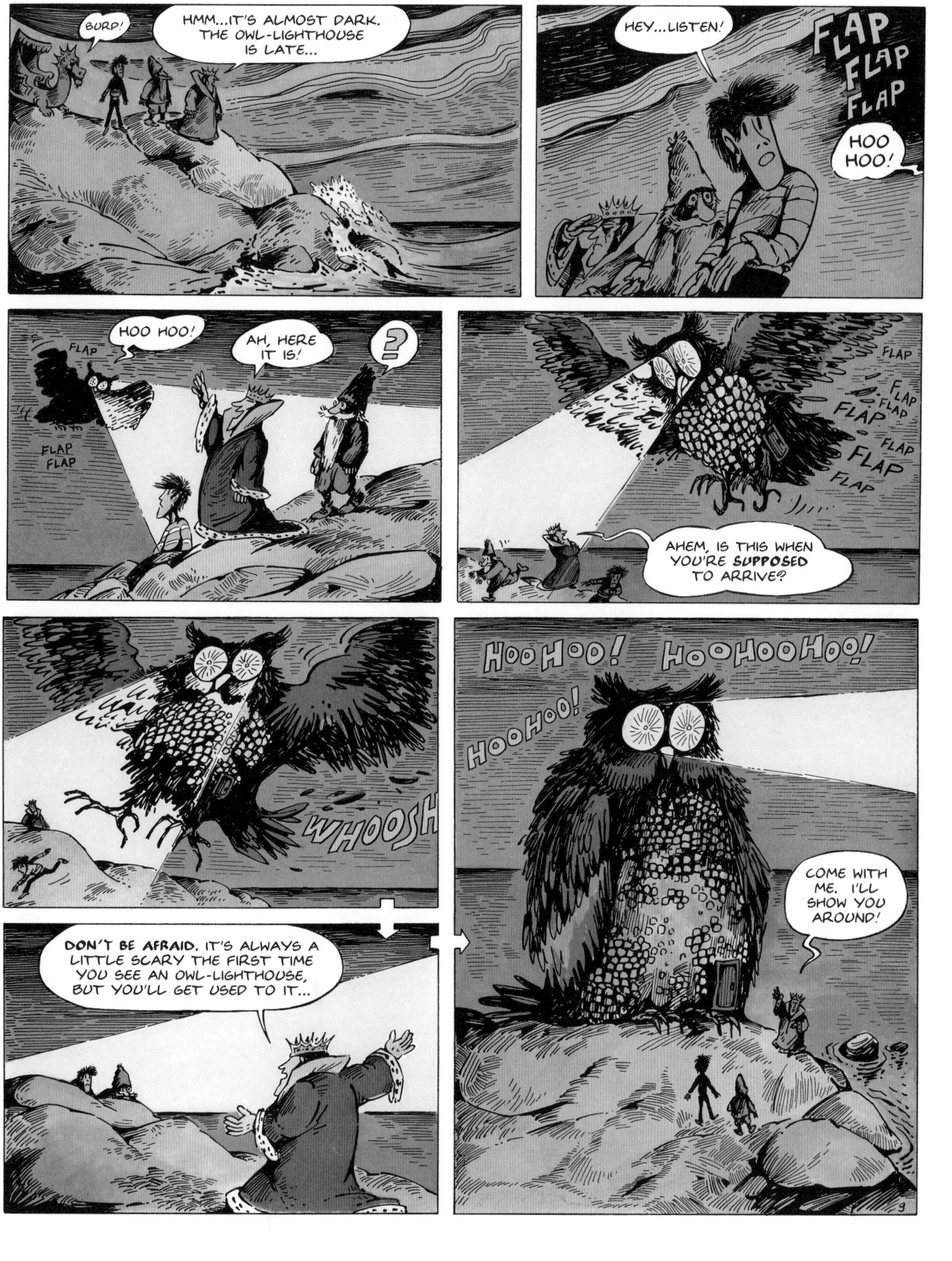
BURP!
HMM...IT'S ALMOST DARK. THE OWL-LIGHTHOUSE IS LATE...
HEY...LISTEN!
FLAP FLAP FLAP
HOO HOO!
HOO HOO!
FLAP
FLAP FLAP
AH, HERE IT IS!
?
FLAP
FLAP FLAP FLAP
FLAP FLAP
FLAP
FLAP
AHEM, IS THIS WHEN YOU'RE SUPPOSED TO ARRIVE?
WHOOSH
HOOHOO! HOOHOOHOO!
HOOHOO!
COME WITH ME. I'LL SHOW YOU AROUND!
DON'T BE AFRAID. IT'S ALWAYS A LITTLE SCARY THE FIRST TIME YOU SEE AN OWL-LIGHTHOUSE, BUT YOU'LL GET USED TO IT...
9

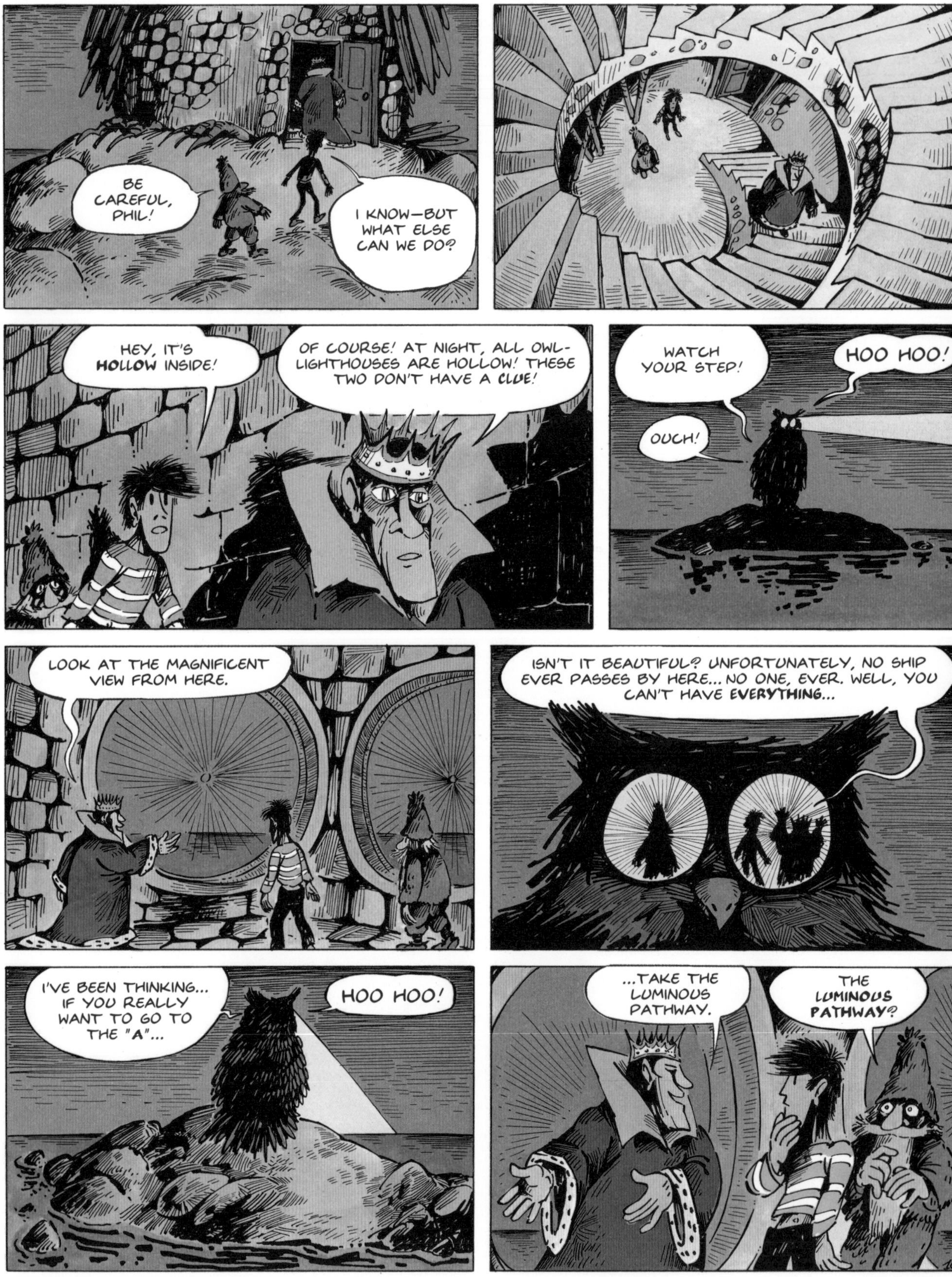
BE CAREFUL, PHIL!
I KNOW—BUT WHAT ELSE CAN WE DO?
HEY, IT'S **HOLLOW** INSIDE!
OF COURSE! AT NIGHT, ALL OWL-LIGHTHOUSES ARE HOLLOW! THESE TWO DON'T HAVE A **CLUE**!
WATCH YOUR STEP!
OUCH!
HOO HOO!
LOOK AT THE MAGNIFICENT VIEW FROM HERE.
ISN'T IT BEAUTIFUL? UNFORTUNATELY, NO SHIP EVER PASSES BY HERE... NO ONE, EVER. WELL, YOU CAN'T HAVE **EVERYTHING**...
I'VE BEEN THINKING... IF YOU REALLY WANT TO GO TO THE "**A**"...
HOO HOO!
...TAKE THE LUMINOUS PATHWAY.
THE **LUMINOUS PATHWAY**?
10

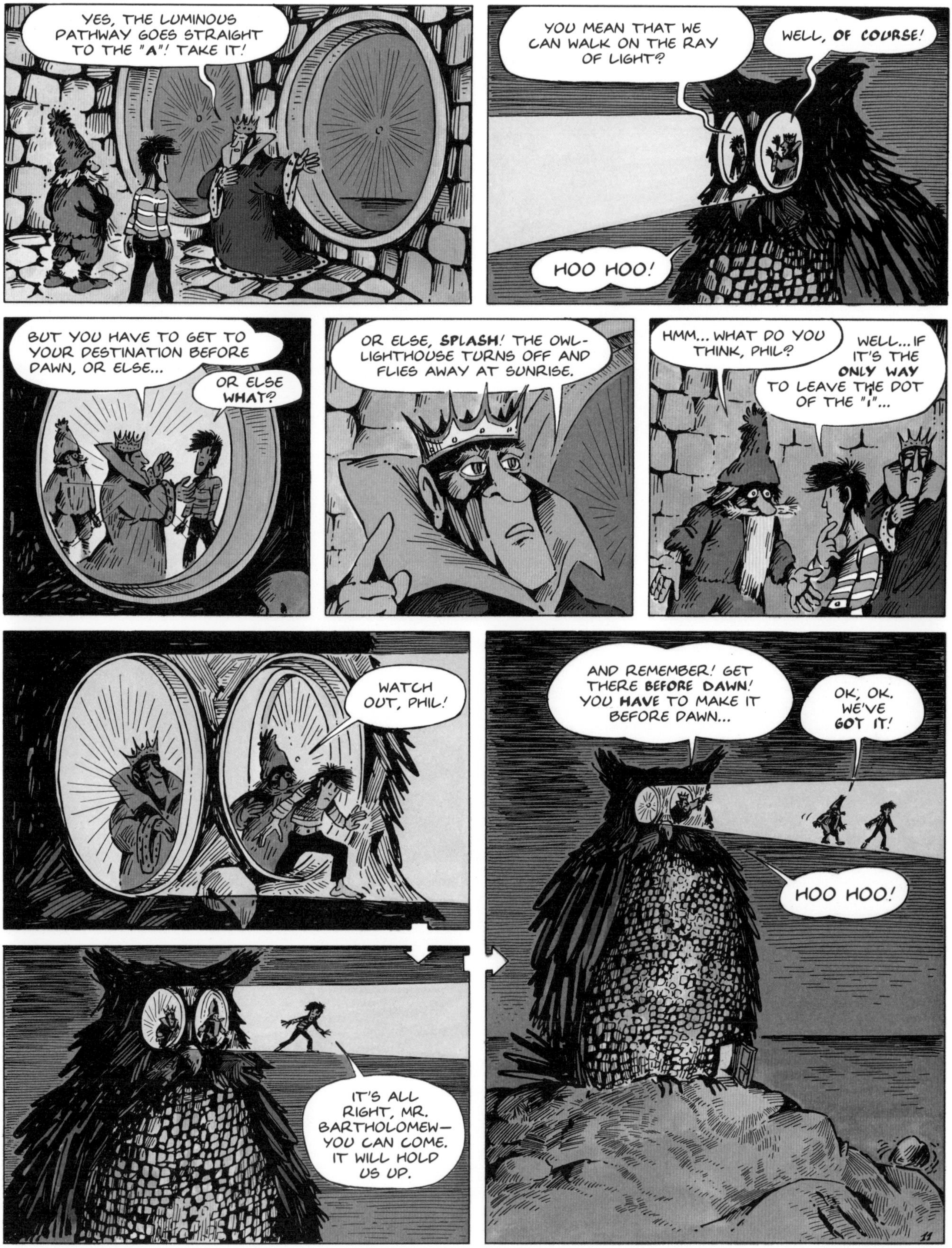
YES, THE LUMINOUS PATHWAY GOES STRAIGHT TO THE "A"! TAKE IT!
YOU MEAN THAT WE CAN WALK ON THE RAY OF LIGHT?
WELL, OF COURSE!
HOO HOO!
BUT YOU HAVE TO GET TO YOUR DESTINATION BEFORE DAWN, OR ELSE...
OR ELSE WHAT?
OR ELSE, SPLASH! THE OWL-LIGHTHOUSE TURNS OFF AND FLIES AWAY AT SUNRISE.
HMM... WHAT DO YOU THINK, PHIL?
WELL... IF IT'S THE ONLY WAY TO LEAVE THE DOT OF THE "I"...
WATCH OUT, PHIL!
IT'S ALL RIGHT, MR. BARTHOLOMEW— YOU CAN COME. IT WILL HOLD US UP.
AND REMEMBER! GET THERE BEFORE DAWN! YOU HAVE TO MAKE IT BEFORE DAWN...
OK, OK. WE'VE GOT IT!
HOO HOO!
11

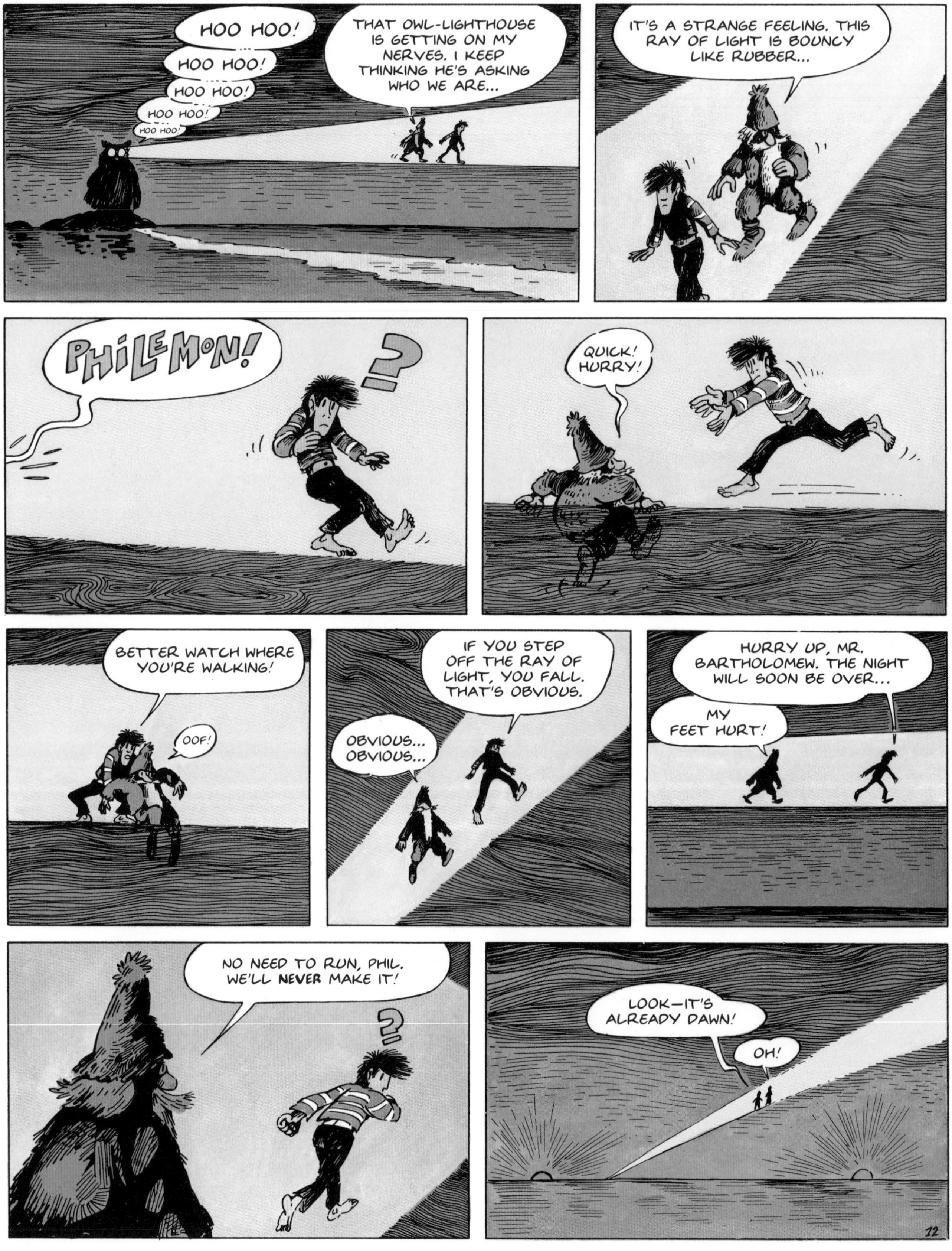
HOO HOO!
HOO HOO!
HOO HOO!
HOO HOO!
HOO HOO!
THAT OWL-LIGHTHOUSE IS GETTING ON MY NERVES. I KEEP THINKING HE'S ASKING WHO WE ARE...
IT'S A STRANGE FEELING. THIS RAY OF LIGHT IS BOUNCY LIKE RUBBER...
PHILEMON!
?
QUICK! HURRY!
BETTER WATCH WHERE YOU'RE WALKING!
OOF!
IF YOU STEP OFF THE RAY OF LIGHT, YOU FALL. THAT'S OBVIOUS.
OBVIOUS... OBVIOUS...
HURRY UP, MR. BARTHOLOMEW. THE NIGHT WILL SOON BE OVER...
MY FEET HURT!
NO NEED TO RUN, PHIL. WE'LL **NEVER** MAKE IT!
?
LOOK—IT'S ALREADY DAWN!
OH!
12

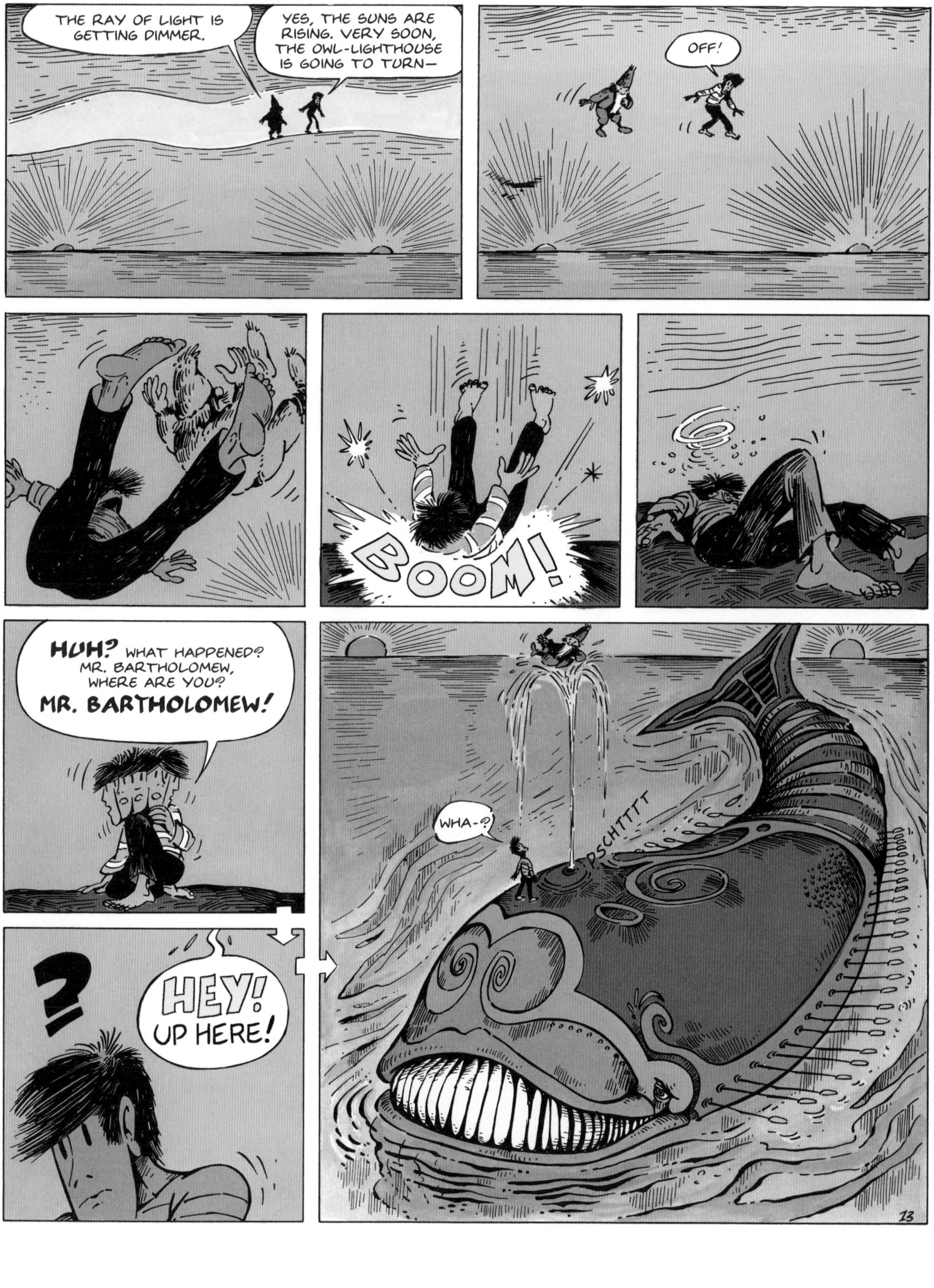
THE RAY OF LIGHT IS GETTING DIMMER.
YES, THE SUNS ARE RISING. VERY SOON, THE OWL-LIGHTHOUSE IS GOING TO TURN—
OFF!
BOOM!
HUH? WHAT HAPPENED? MR. BARTHOLOMEW, WHERE ARE YOU? MR. BARTHOLOMEW!
?
HEY! UP HERE!
WHA-?
PSCHTTTT
13

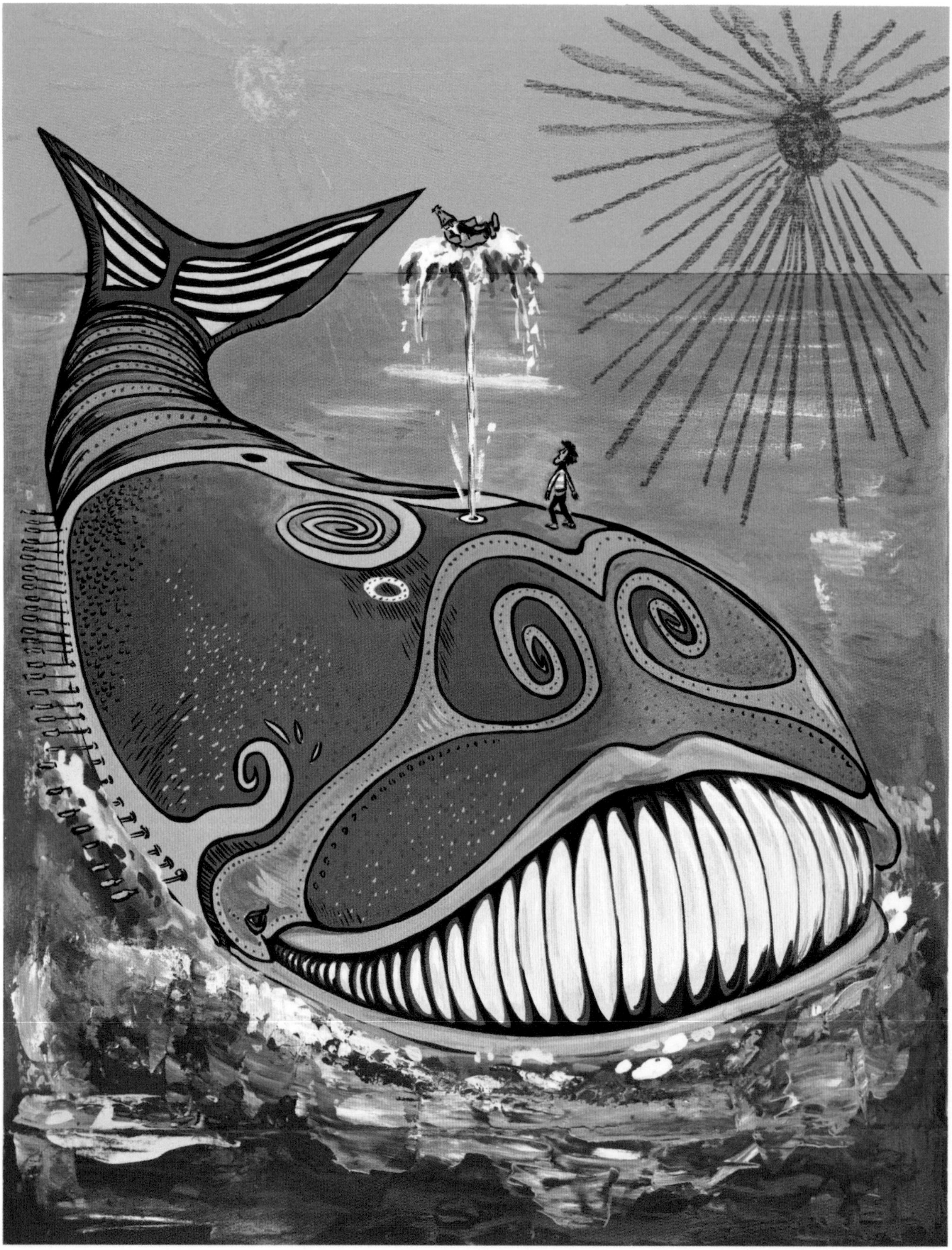

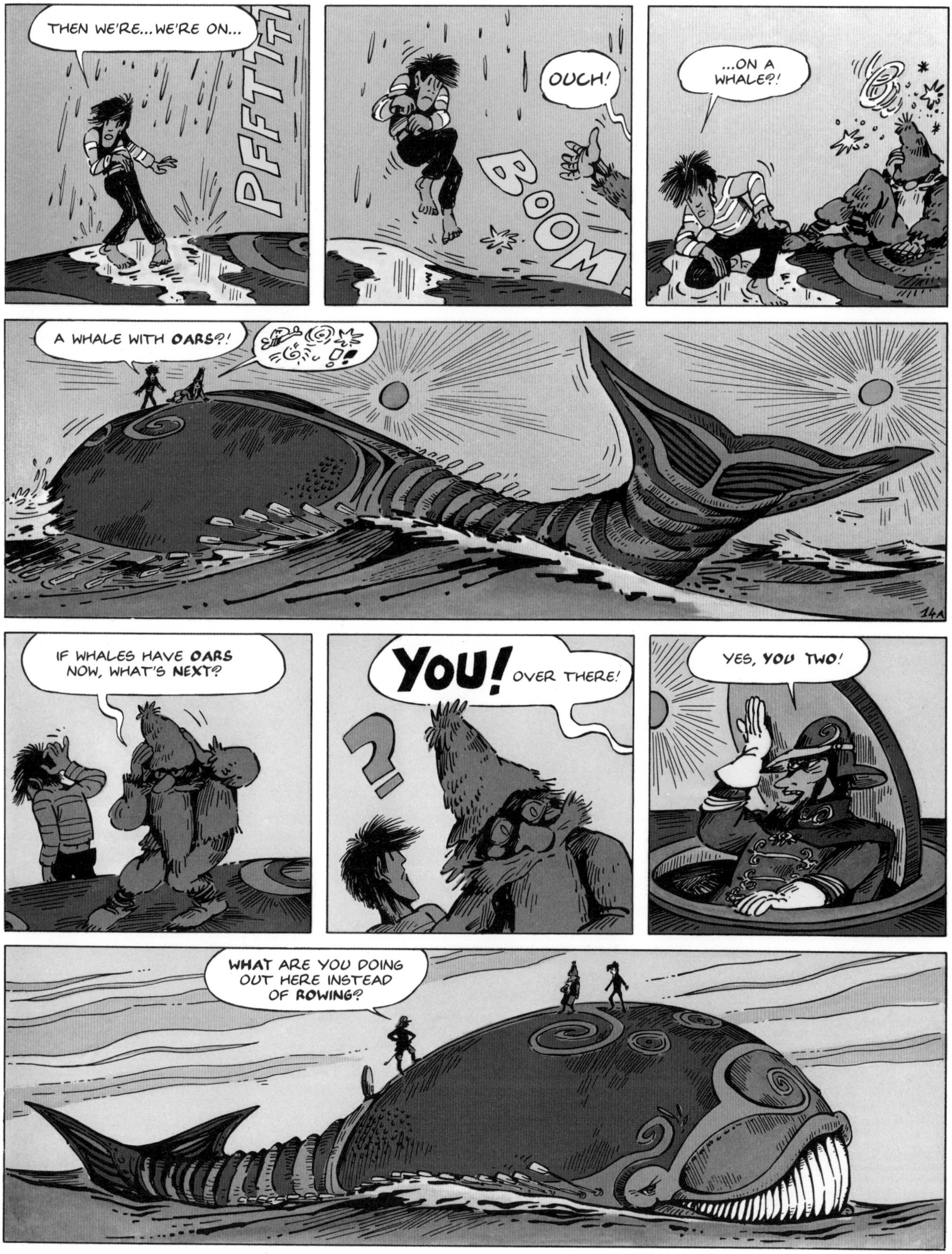
THEN WE'RE... WE'RE ON...
PFFTTT
OUCH!
BOOM
...ON A WHALE?!
A WHALE WITH OARS?!
14A
IF WHALES HAVE OARS NOW, WHAT'S NEXT?
YOU! OVER THERE!
YES, YOU TWO!
WHAT ARE YOU DOING OUT HERE INSTEAD OF ROWING?

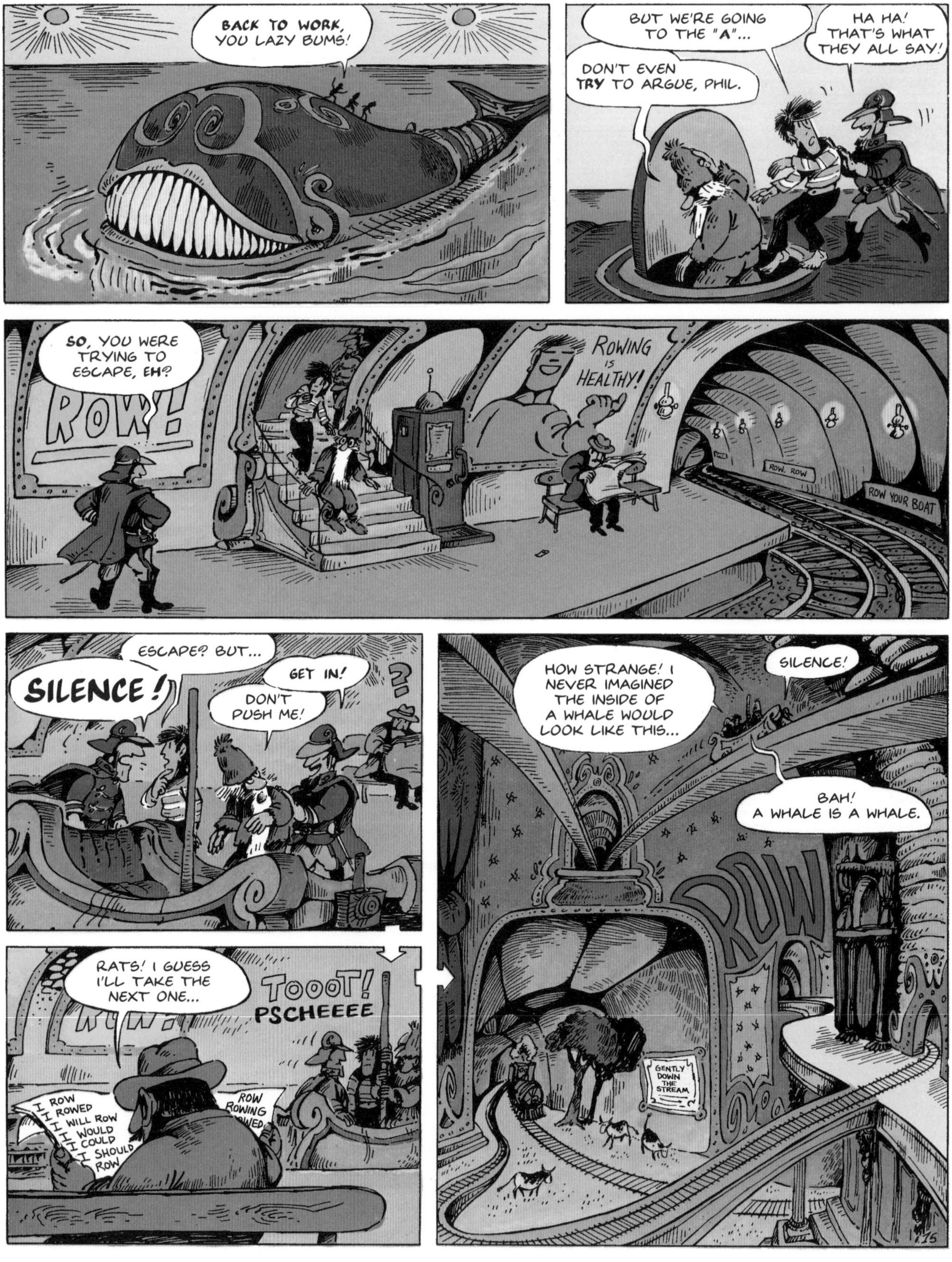
BACK TO WORK, YOU LAZY BUMS!
BUT WE'RE GOING TO THE "A"...
HA HA! THAT'S WHAT THEY ALL SAY!
DON'T EVEN TRY TO ARGUE, PHIL.
SO, YOU WERE TRYING TO ESCAPE, EH?
ROW!
ROWING IS HEALTHY!
ROW. ROW
ROW YOUR BOAT
ESCAPE? BUT...
SILENCE!
GET IN!
DON'T PUSH ME!
?
RATS! I GUESS I'LL TAKE THE NEXT ONE...
TOOOT!
PSCHEEEE
I ROW
I ROWED
I WILL ROW
I WOULD
I COULD
I SHOULD ROW
ROW
ROWING
ROWED
HOW STRANGE! I NEVER IMAGINED THE INSIDE OF A WHALE WOULD LOOK LIKE THIS...
SILENCE!
BAH! A WHALE IS A WHALE.
ROW
GENTLY DOWN THE STREAM

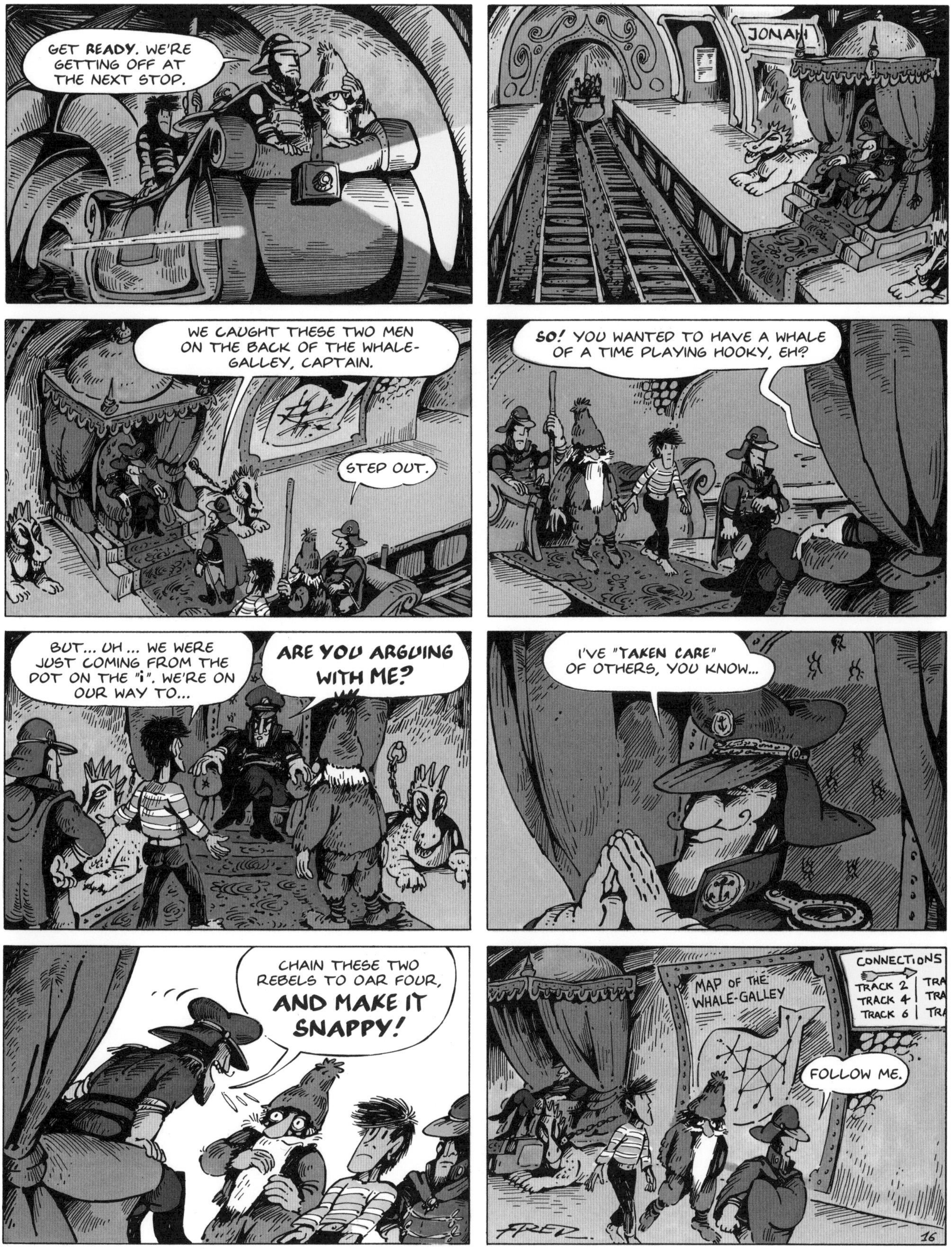
GET READY. WE'RE GETTING OFF AT THE NEXT STOP.
JONAH
WE CAUGHT THESE TWO MEN ON THE BACK OF THE WHALE-GALLEY, CAPTAIN.
STEP OUT.
SO! YOU WANTED TO HAVE A WHALE OF A TIME PLAYING HOOKY, EH?
BUT... UH ... WE WERE JUST COMING FROM THE DOT ON THE "i". WE'RE ON OUR WAY TO...
ARE YOU ARGUING WITH ME?
I'VE "TAKEN CARE" OF OTHERS, YOU KNOW...
CHAIN THESE TWO REBELS TO OAR FOUR, AND MAKE IT SNAPPY!
CONNECTIONS
TRACK 2
TRACK 4
TRACK 6
MAP OF THE WHALE-GALLEY
FOLLOW ME.
FRED
16

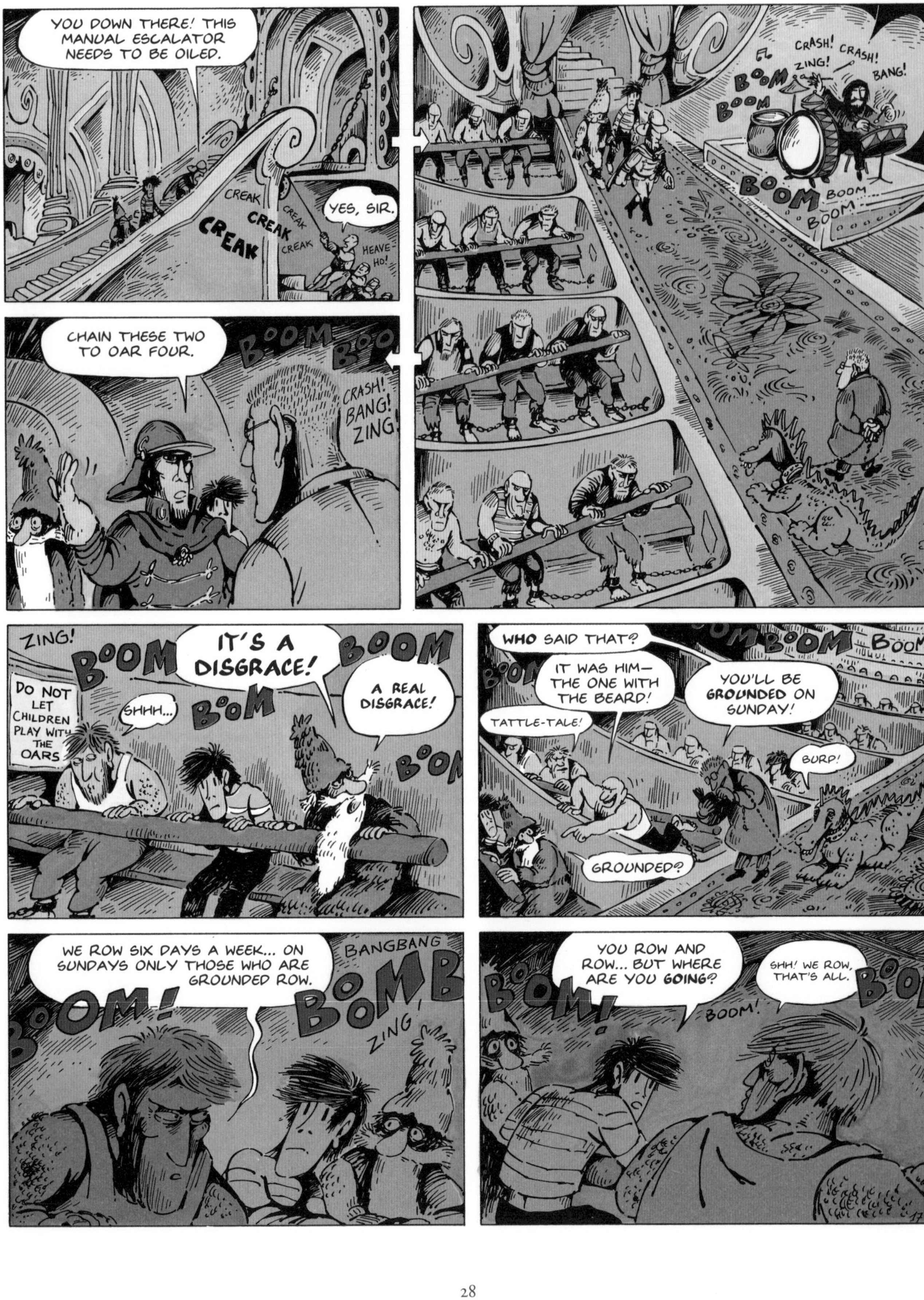
YOU DOWN THERE! THIS MANUAL ESCALATOR NEEDS TO BE OILED.
CREAK CREAK CREAK
CREAK CREAK CREAK
YES, SIR.
HEAVE-HO!
CRASH! CRASH! ZING! BANG!
BOOM BOOM
BOOM BOOM BOOM
CHAIN THESE TWO TO OAR FOUR.
BOOM BOO
CRASH! BANG! ZING!
ZING!
BOOM
IT'S A DISGRACE!
BOOM
DO NOT LET CHILDREN PLAY WITH THE OARS
SHHH...
BOOM
A REAL DISGRACE!
BOOM
WHO SAID THAT?
BOOM BOOM BOOM
IT WAS HIM— THE ONE WITH THE BEARD!
YOU'LL BE GROUNDED ON SUNDAY!
TATTLE-TALE!
BURP!
GROUNDED?
WE ROW SIX DAYS A WEEK... ON SUNDAYS ONLY THOSE WHO ARE GROUNDED ROW.
BANGBANG
BOOM!
BOMB
ZING
YOU ROW AND ROW... BUT WHERE ARE YOU GOING?
SHH! WE ROW, THAT'S ALL.
BOOM!
BOOM
BOOM

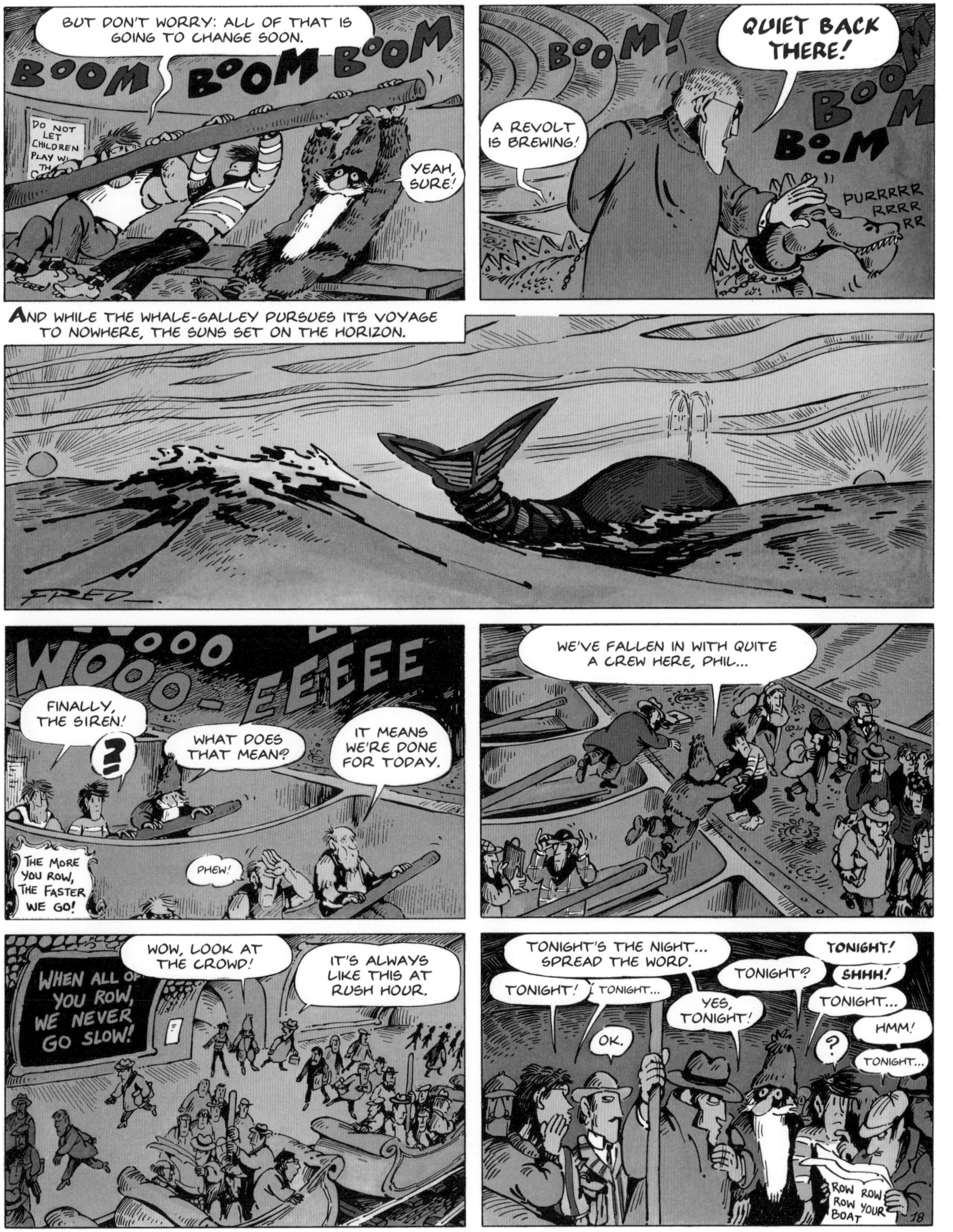
BUT DON'T WORRY: ALL OF THAT IS GOING TO CHANGE SOON.
BOOM BOOM BOOM
DO NOT LET CHILDREN PLAY WI
YEAH, SURE!
BOOM!
QUIET BACK THERE!
A REVOLT IS BREWING!
BOOM BOOM
PURRRRR RRRR RR
AND WHILE THE WHALE-GALLEY PURSUES ITS VOYAGE TO NOWHERE, THE SUNS SET ON THE HORIZON.
FRED
WOOO-EEEEE
FINALLY, THE SIREN!
?
WHAT DOES THAT MEAN?
IT MEANS WE'RE DONE FOR TODAY.
THE MORE YOU ROW, THE FASTER WE GO!
PHEW!
WE'VE FALLEN IN WITH QUITE A CREW HERE, PHIL...
WHEN ALL OF YOU ROW, WE NEVER GO SLOW!
WOW, LOOK AT THE CROWD!
IT'S ALWAYS LIKE THIS AT RUSH HOUR.
TONIGHT'S THE NIGHT... SPREAD THE WORD.
TONIGHT!
TONIGHT...
OK.
YES, TONIGHT!
TONIGHT?
TONIGHT!
SHHH!
TONIGHT...
?
HMM!
TONIGHT...
ROW ROW ROW YOUR BOAT
18

GENTLY ROCKED BY THE OCEAN WAVES, THE WHALE-GALLEY DRIFTS OFF TO SLEEP BENEATH THE TWO MOONS.

INSIDE, THE CAPTAIN IS SNORING AS ONLY THE CAPTAIN OF A WHALE-GALLEY CAN...

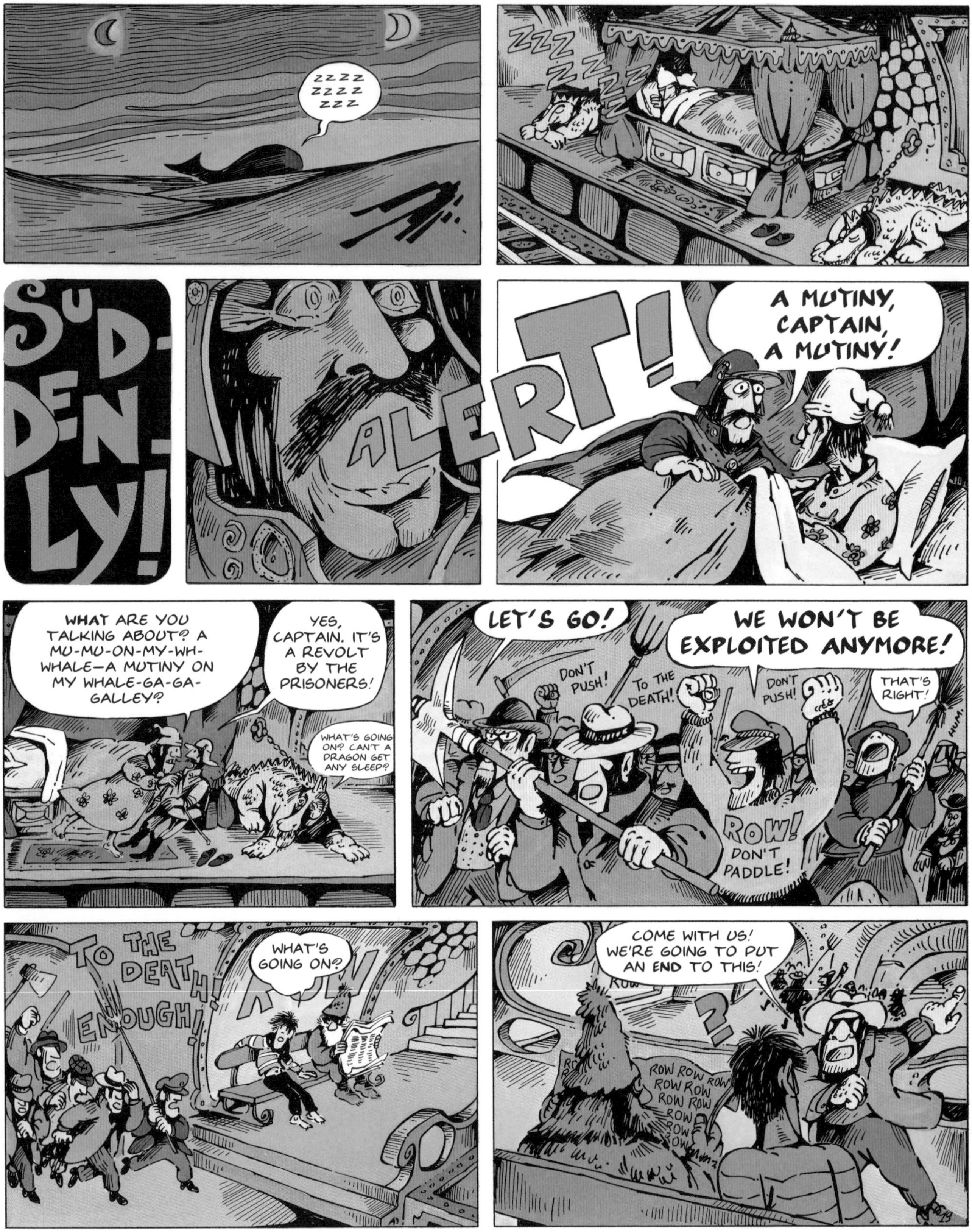

ZZZZ ZZZZ ZZZ
ZZZZZZZZ
SUD-DEN-LY!
ALERT!
A MUTINY, CAPTAIN, A MUTINY!
WHAT ARE YOU TALKING ABOUT? A MU-MU-ON-MY-WH-WHALE—A MUTINY ON MY WHALE-GA-GA-GALLEY?
YES, CAPTAIN. IT'S A REVOLT BY THE PRISONERS!
WHAT'S GOING ON? CAN'T A DRAGON GET ANY SLEEP?
LET'S GO!
WE WON'T BE EXPLOITED ANYMORE!
DON'T PUSH!
TO THE DEATH!
DON'T PUSH!
THAT'S RIGHT!
HUM.
ROW! DON'T PADDLE!
TO THE DEATH!
ENOUGH!
WHAT'S GOING ON?
ROW
COME WITH US! WE'RE GOING TO PUT AN END TO THIS!
ROW
?
ROW ROW ROW ROW ROW ROW ROW ROW ROW ROW ROW

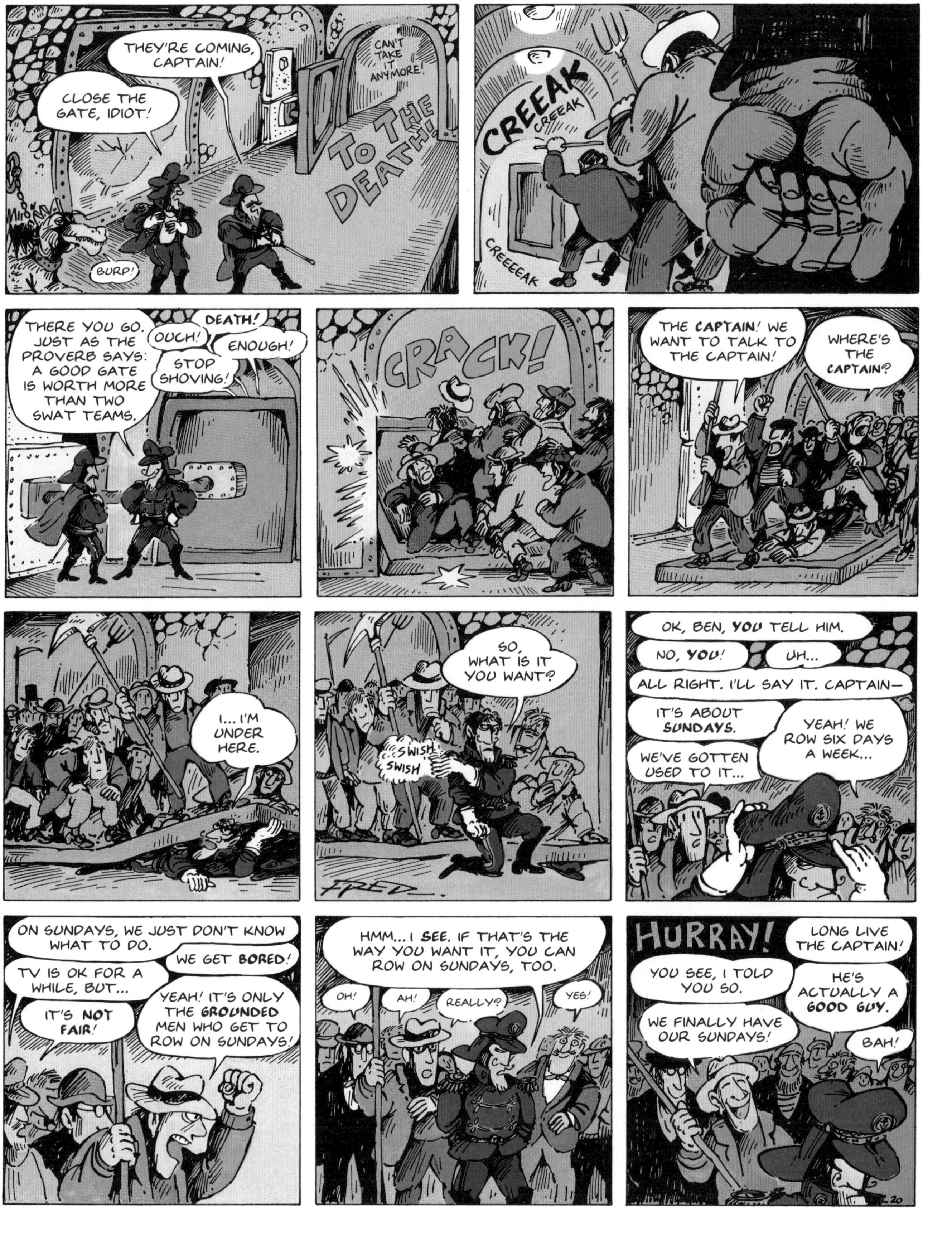
THEY'RE COMING, CAPTAIN!
CLOSE THE GATE, IDIOT!
CAN'T TAKE IT ANYMORE!
TO THE DEATH!
BURP!
CREEAK
CREEAK
CREEEEAK
THERE YOU GO. JUST AS THE PROVERB SAYS: A GOOD GATE IS WORTH MORE THAN TWO SWAT TEAMS.
DEATH!
OUCH!
ENOUGH!
STOP SHOVING!
CRACK!
THE CAPTAIN! WE WANT TO TALK TO THE CAPTAIN!
WHERE'S THE CAPTAIN?
I... I'M UNDER HERE.
SO, WHAT IS IT YOU WANT?
SWISH
SWISH
FRED
OK, BEN, YOU TELL HIM.
NO, YOU!
UH...
ALL RIGHT. I'LL SAY IT. CAPTAIN—
IT'S ABOUT SUNDAYS.
WE'VE GOTTEN USED TO IT...
YEAH! WE ROW SIX DAYS A WEEK...
ON SUNDAYS, WE JUST DON'T KNOW WHAT TO DO.
WE GET BORED!
TV IS OK FOR A WHILE, BUT...
IT'S NOT FAIR!
YEAH! IT'S ONLY THE GROUNDED MEN WHO GET TO ROW ON SUNDAYS!
HMM... I SEE. IF THAT'S THE WAY YOU WANT IT, YOU CAN ROW ON SUNDAYS, TOO.
OH!
AH!
REALLY?
YES!
HURRAY!
LONG LIVE THE CAPTAIN!
YOU SEE, I TOLD YOU SO.
HE'S ACTUALLY A GOOD GUY.
WE FINALLY HAVE OUR SUNDAYS!
BAH!
20

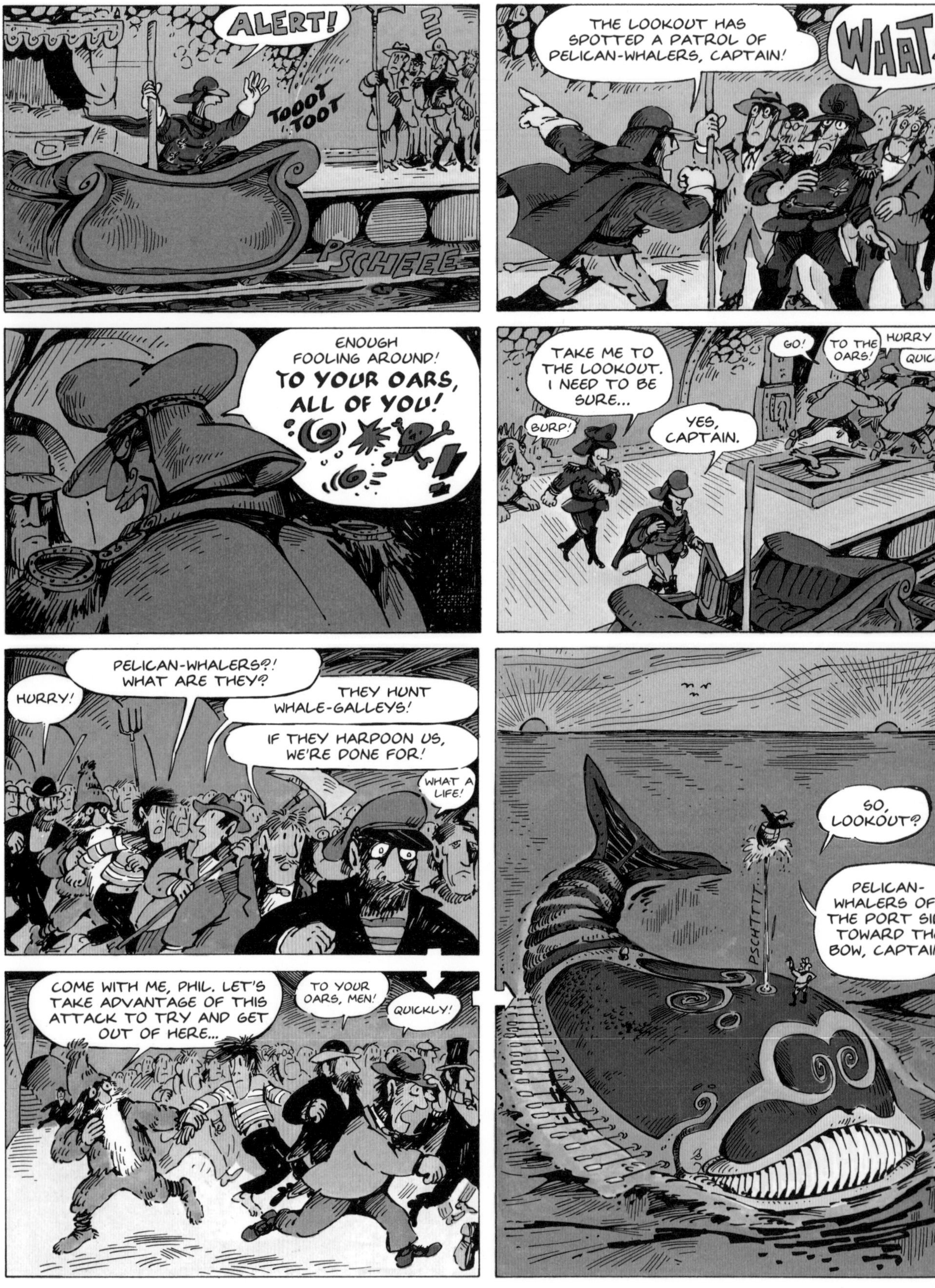
ALERT!
TOOOT TOOT
PSCHEEE
THE LOOKOUT HAS SPOTTED A PATROL OF PELICAN-WHALERS, CAPTAIN!
WHAT!?
ENOUGH FOOLING AROUND! TO YOUR OARS, ALL OF YOU!
TAKE ME TO THE LOOKOUT. I NEED TO BE SURE...
BURP!
YES, CAPTAIN.
GO!
TO THE OARS!
HURRY UP!
QUICKLY!
PELICAN-WHALERS?! WHAT ARE THEY?
HURRY!
THEY HUNT WHALE-GALLEYS!
IF THEY HARPOON US, WE'RE DONE FOR!
WHAT A LIFE!
COME WITH ME, PHIL. LET'S TAKE ADVANTAGE OF THIS ATTACK TO TRY AND GET OUT OF HERE...
TO YOUR OARS, MEN!
QUICKLY!
SO, LOOKOUT?
PELICAN-WHALERS OFF THE PORT SIDE TOWARD THE BOW, CAPTAIN!
PSCHTTTT
21

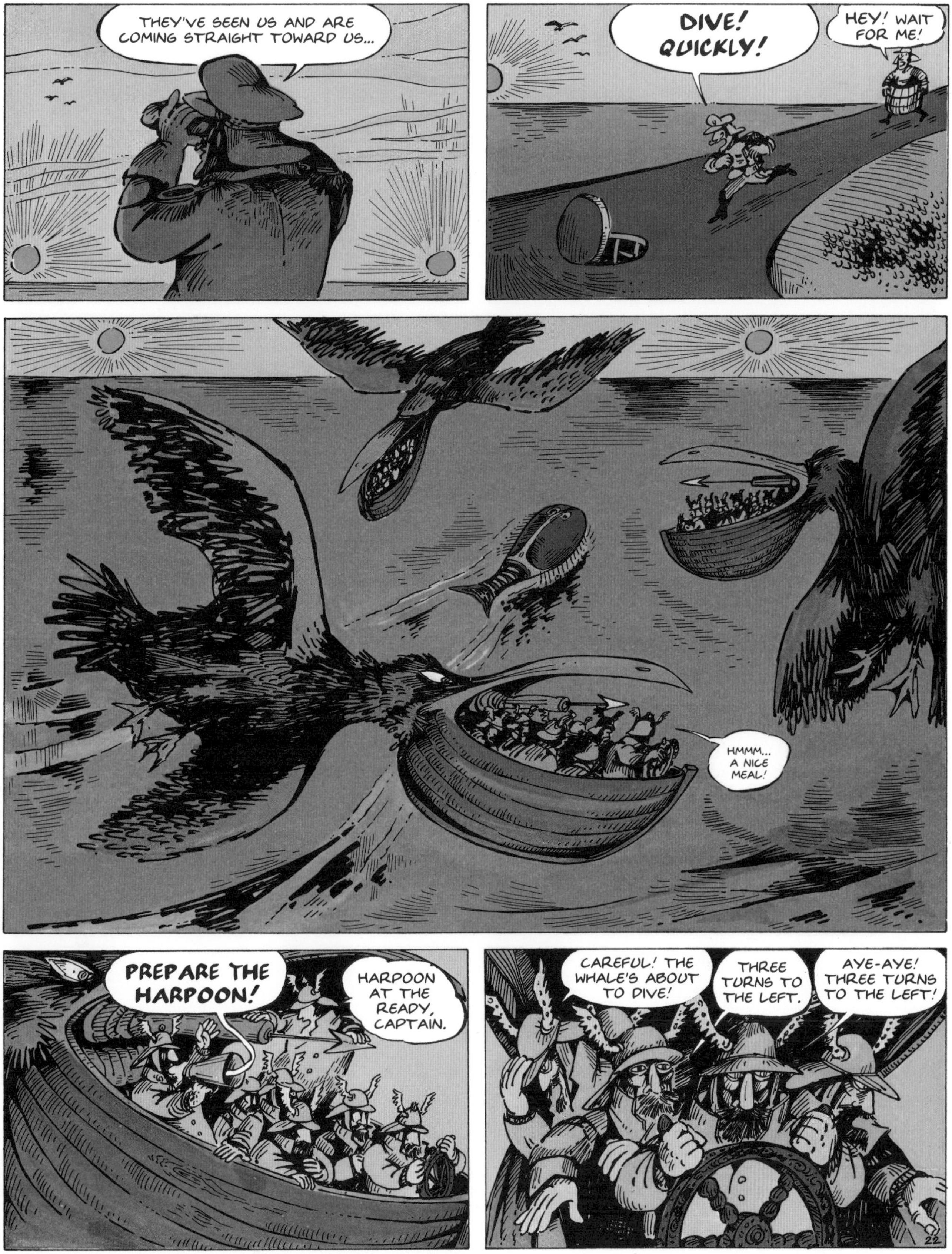

THEY'VE SEEN US AND ARE COMING STRAIGHT TOWARD US...
DIVE! QUICKLY!
HEY! WAIT FOR ME!
HMMM... A NICE MEAL!
PREPARE THE HARPOON!
HARPOON AT THE READY, CAPTAIN.
CAREFUL! THE WHALE'S ABOUT TO DIVE!
THREE TURNS TO THE LEFT.
AYE-AYE! THREE TURNS TO THE LEFT!
22

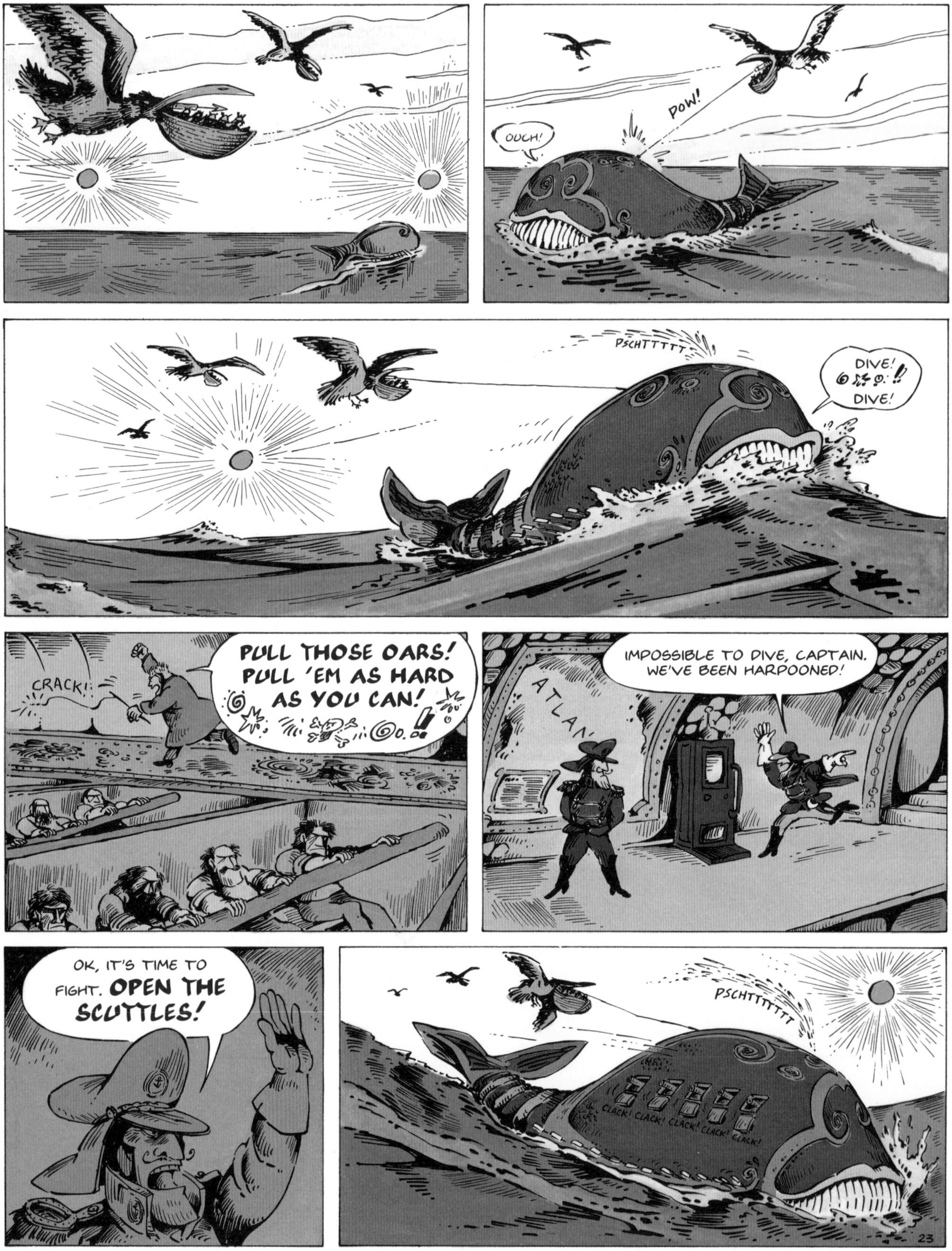

POW!
OUCH!
PSCHTTTTTT
DIVE!
DIVE!
CRACK!
PULL THOSE OARS! PULL 'EM AS HARD AS YOU CAN!
ATLAN
IMPOSSIBLE TO DIVE, CAPTAIN. WE'VE BEEN HARPOONED!
OK, IT'S TIME TO FIGHT. OPEN THE SCUTTLES!
PSCHTTTTTTT
CLACK! CLACK! CLACK! CLACK! CLACK!
23

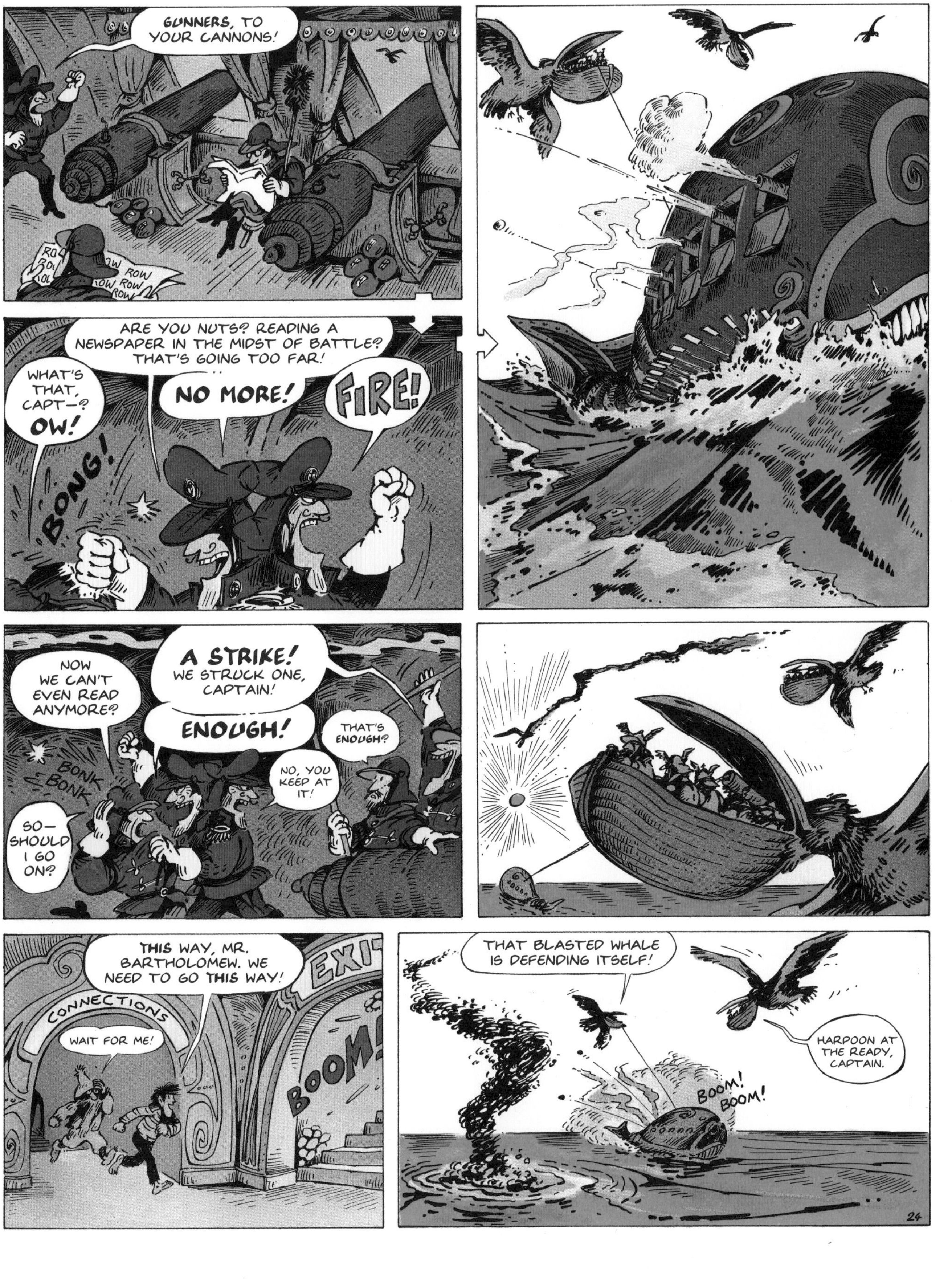
GUNNERS, TO YOUR CANNONS!
ARE YOU NUTS? READING A NEWSPAPER IN THE MIDST OF BATTLE? THAT'S GOING TOO FAR!
WHAT'S THAT, CAPT—? OW!
NO MORE!
FIRE!
BONG!
NOW WE CAN'T EVEN READ ANYMORE?
A STRIKE! WE STRUCK ONE, CAPTAIN!
ENOUGH!
THAT'S ENOUGH?
NO, YOU KEEP AT IT!
BONK BONK
SO— SHOULD I GO ON?
THIS WAY, MR. BARTHOLOMEW. WE NEED TO GO THIS WAY!
CONNECTIONS
EXIT
WAIT FOR ME!
BOOM!
THAT BLASTED WHALE IS DEFENDING ITSELF!
HARPOON AT THE READY, CAPTAIN.
BOOM! BOOM!
24

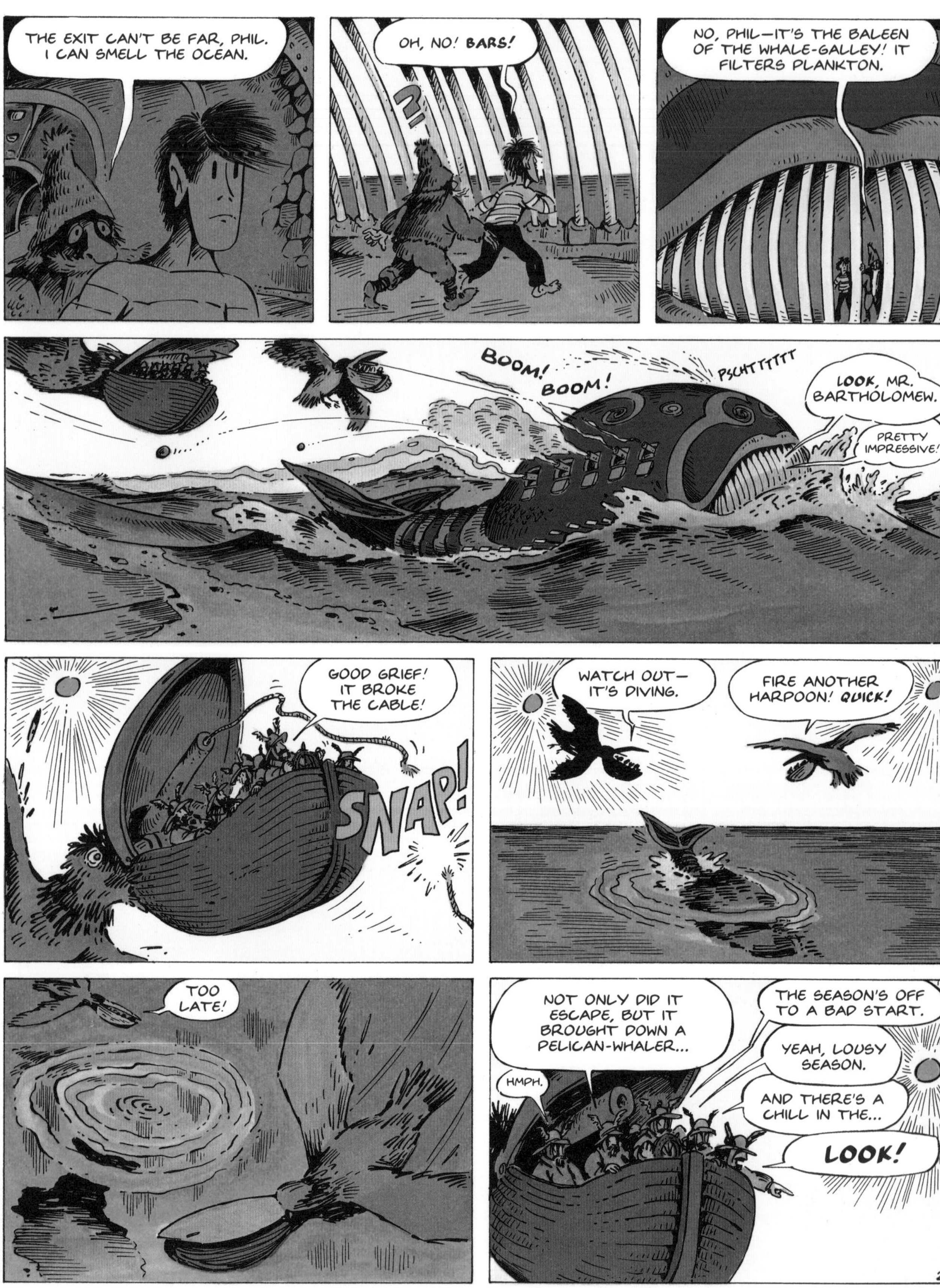
THE EXIT CAN'T BE FAR, PHIL. I CAN SMELL THE OCEAN.
OH, NO! **BARS!**
?
NO, PHIL—IT'S THE BALEEN OF THE WHALE-GALLEY! IT FILTERS PLANKTON.
BOOM!
BOOM!
PSCHTTTTTT
LOOK, MR. BARTHOLOMEW.
PRETTY IMPRESSIVE!
GOOD GRIEF! IT BROKE THE CABLE!
SNAP!
WATCH OUT— IT'S DIVING.
FIRE ANOTHER HARPOON! ***QUICK!***
TOO LATE!
NOT ONLY DID IT ESCAPE, BUT IT BROUGHT DOWN A PELICAN-WHALER...
HMPH.
THE SEASON'S OFF TO A BAD START.
YEAH, LOUSY SEASON.
AND THERE'S A CHILL IN THE...
LOOK!
25

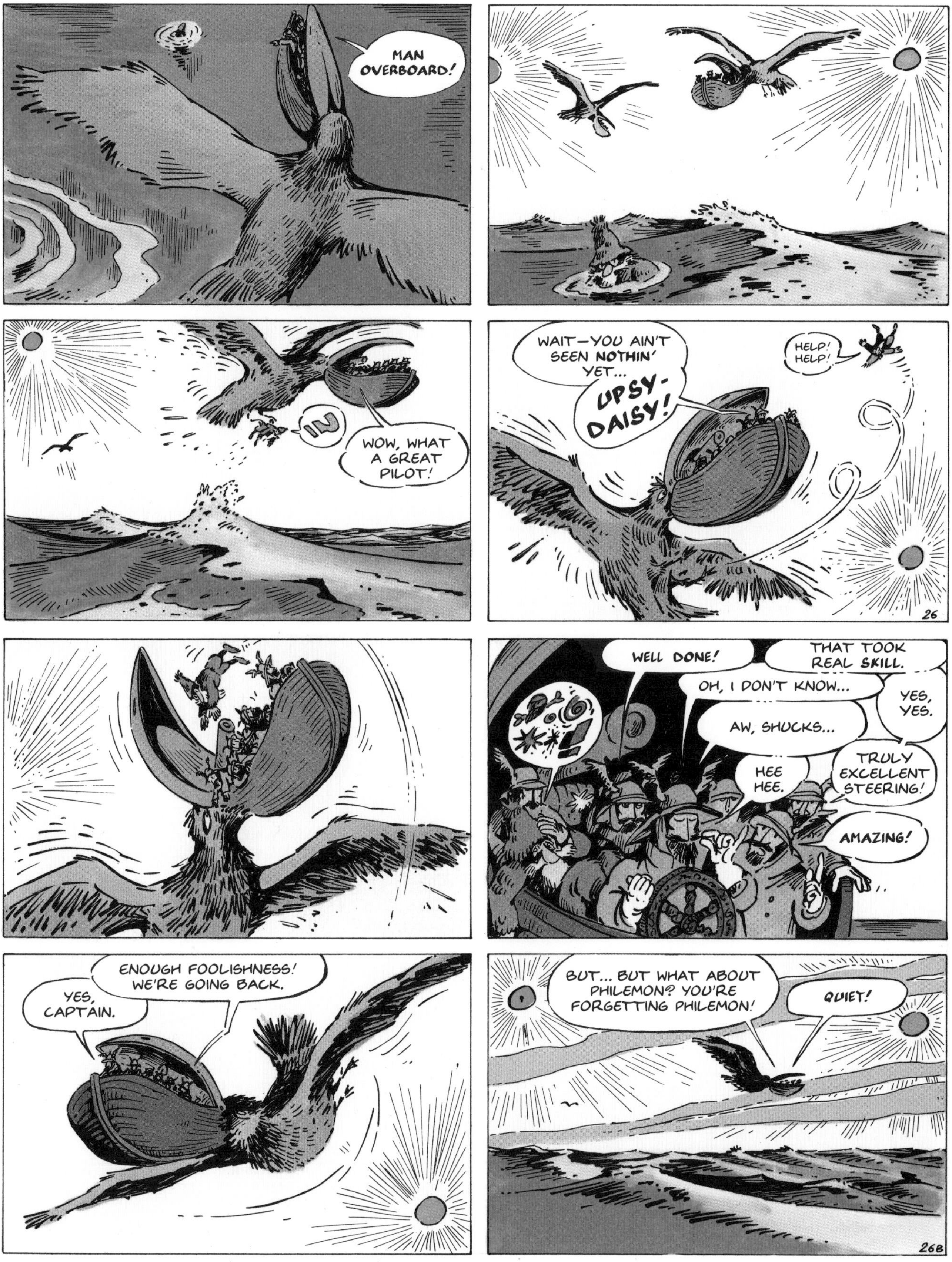

MAN OVERBOARD!
WAIT—YOU AIN'T SEEN NOTHIN' YET... UPSY-DAISY!
WOW, WHAT A GREAT PILOT!
HELP! HELP!
26
WELL DONE!
THAT TOOK REAL SKILL.
OH, I DON'T KNOW...
YES, YES.
AW, SHUCKS...
HEE HEE.
TRULY EXCELLENT STEERING!
AMAZING!
ENOUGH FOOLISHNESS! WE'RE GOING BACK.
YES, CAPTAIN.
BUT... BUT WHAT ABOUT PHILEMON? YOU'RE FORGETTING PHILEMON!
QUIET!
26B

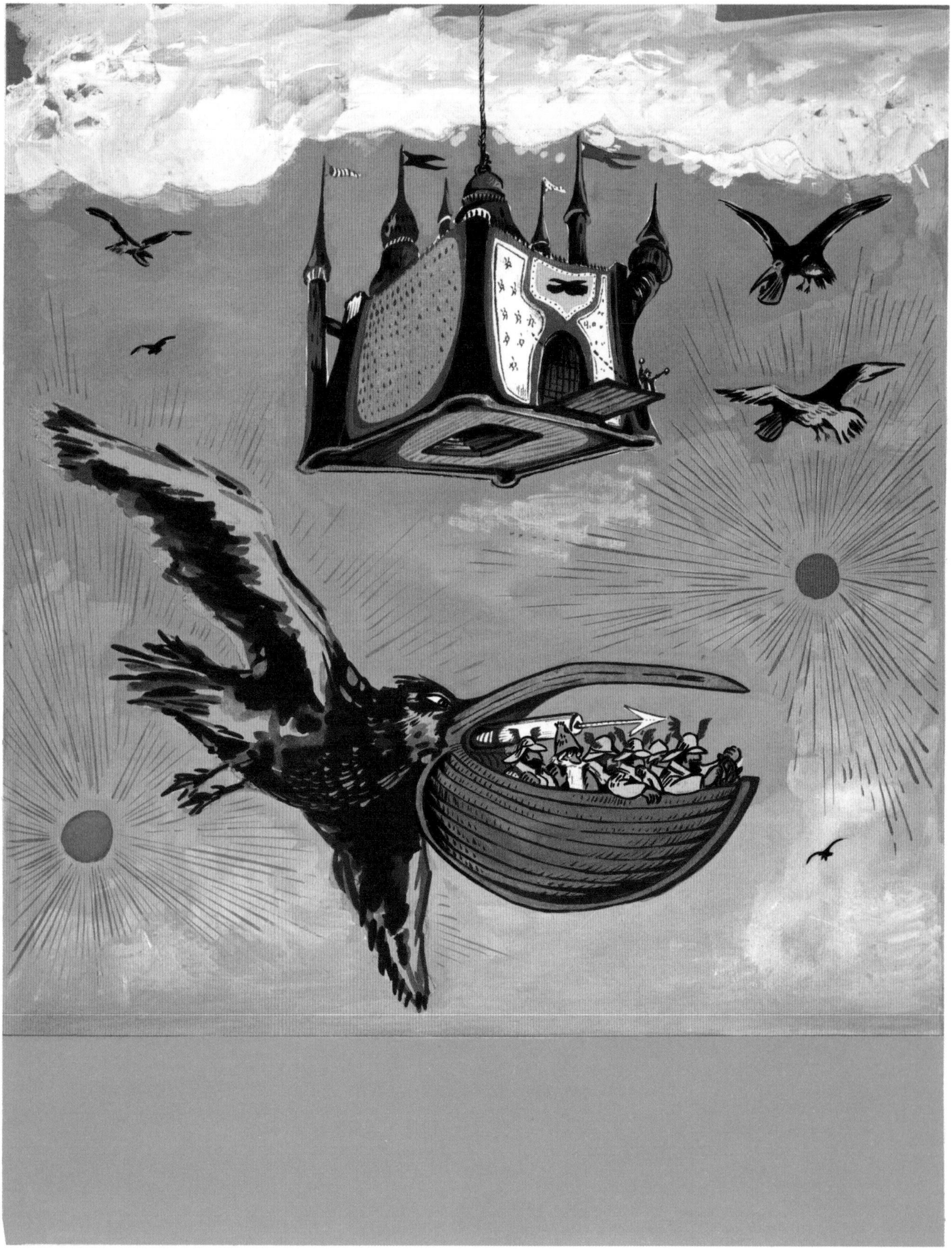

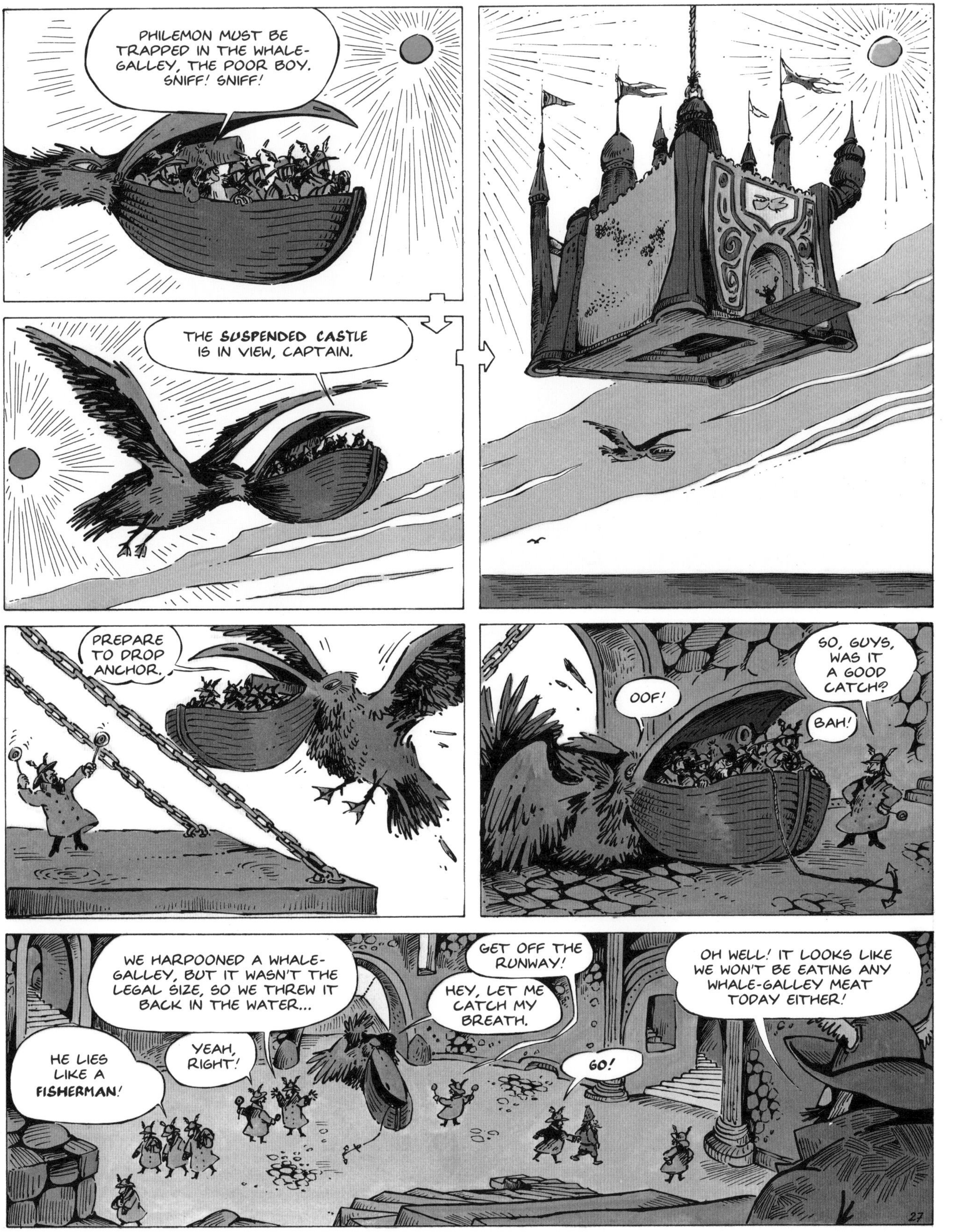
PHILEMON MUST BE TRAPPED IN THE WHALE-GALLEY, THE POOR BOY. SNIFF! SNIFF!
THE **SUSPENDED CASTLE** IS IN VIEW, CAPTAIN.
PREPARE TO DROP ANCHOR.
OOF!
SO, GUYS, WAS IT A GOOD CATCH?
BAH!
WE HARPOONED A WHALE-GALLEY, BUT IT WASN'T THE LEGAL SIZE, SO WE THREW IT BACK IN THE WATER...
HE LIES LIKE A **FISHERMAN**!
YEAH, RIGHT!
GET OFF THE RUNWAY!
HEY, LET ME CATCH MY BREATH.
GO!
OH WELL! IT LOOKS LIKE WE WON'T BE EATING ANY WHALE-GALLEY MEAT TODAY EITHER!
27

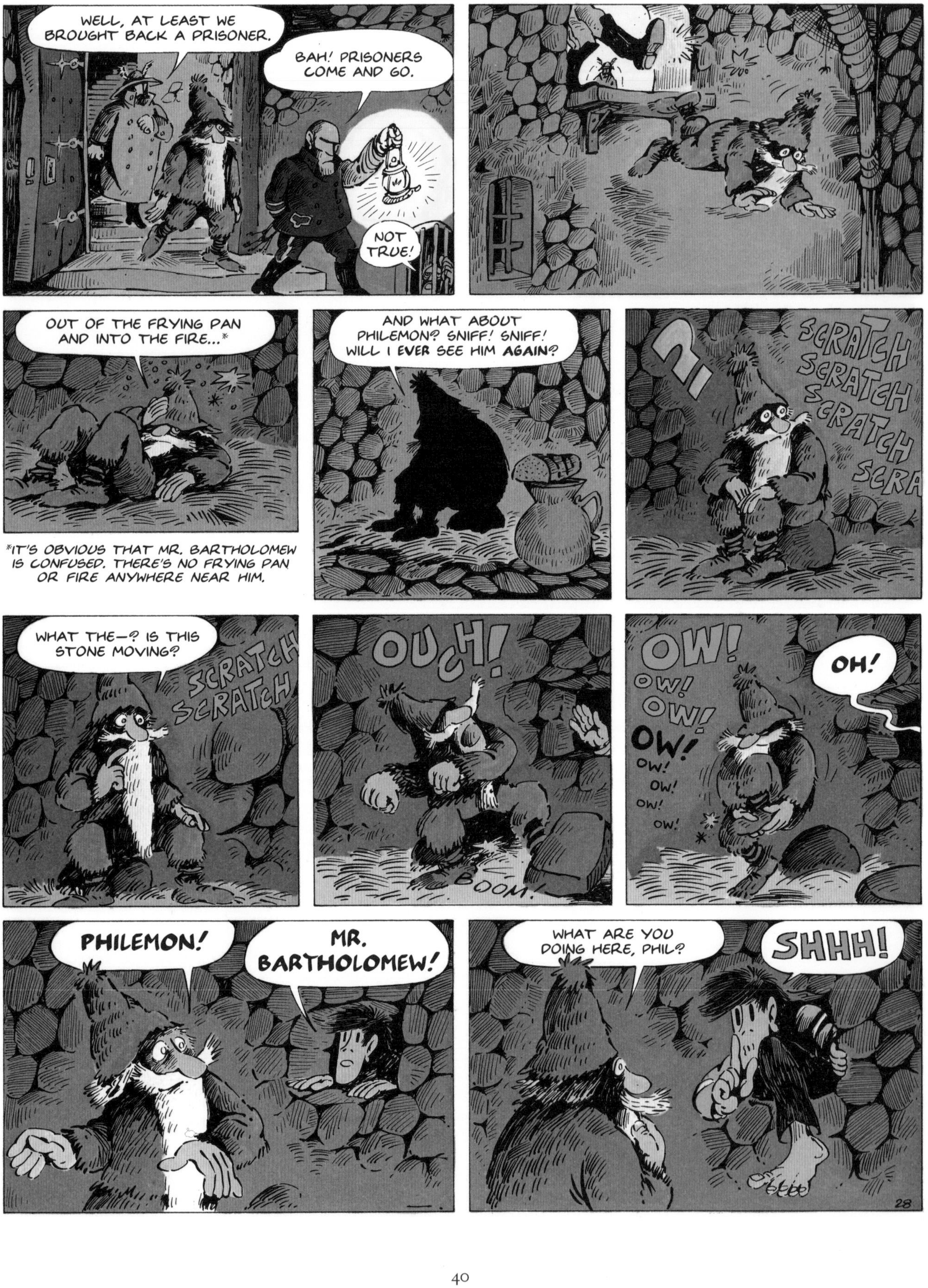
WELL, AT LEAST WE BROUGHT BACK A PRISONER.
BAH! PRISONERS COME AND GO.
NOT TRUE!
OUT OF THE FRYING PAN AND INTO THE FIRE...*
AND WHAT ABOUT PHILEMON? SNIFF! SNIFF! WILL I **EVER** SEE HIM **AGAIN**?
?
SCRATCH SCRATCH SCRATCH SCRATCH SCRA
WHAT THE—? IS THIS STONE MOVING?
SCRATCH SCRATCH
OUCH!
BOOM
OW! OW! OW! OW! OW! OW! OW! OW!
OH!
PHILEMON!
MR. BARTHOLOMEW!
WHAT ARE YOU DOING HERE, PHIL?
SHHH!
28

*IT'S OBVIOUS THAT MR. BARTHOLOMEW IS CONFUSED. THERE'S NO FRYING PAN OR FIRE ANYWHERE NEAR HIM.

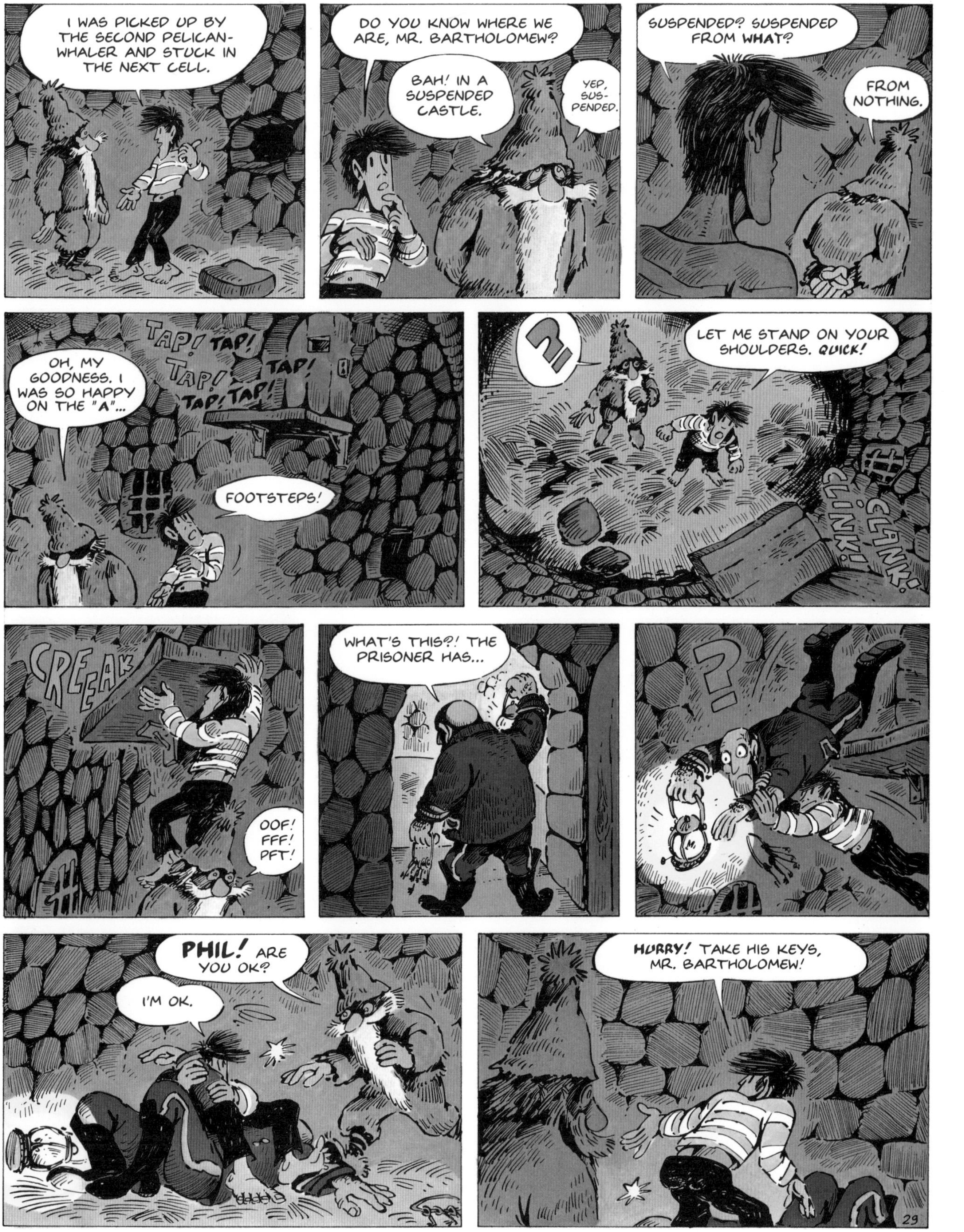
I WAS PICKED UP BY THE SECOND PELICAN-WHALER AND STUCK IN THE NEXT CELL.
DO YOU KNOW WHERE WE ARE, MR. BARTHOLOMEW?
BAH! IN A SUSPENDED CASTLE.
YEP, SUS-PENDED.
SUSPENDED? SUSPENDED FROM **WHAT**?
FROM NOTHING.
TAP! TAP! TAP! TAP! TAP! TAP!
OH, MY GOODNESS. I WAS SO HAPPY ON THE "**A**"...
FOOTSTEPS!
?!
LET ME STAND ON YOUR SHOULDERS. ***QUICK!***
CLINK! CLANK!
CREEAK
OOF! FFF! PFT!
WHAT'S THIS?! THE PRISONER HAS...
?!
PHIL! ARE YOU OK?
I'M OK.
HURRY! TAKE HIS KEYS, MR. BARTHOLOMEW!
29

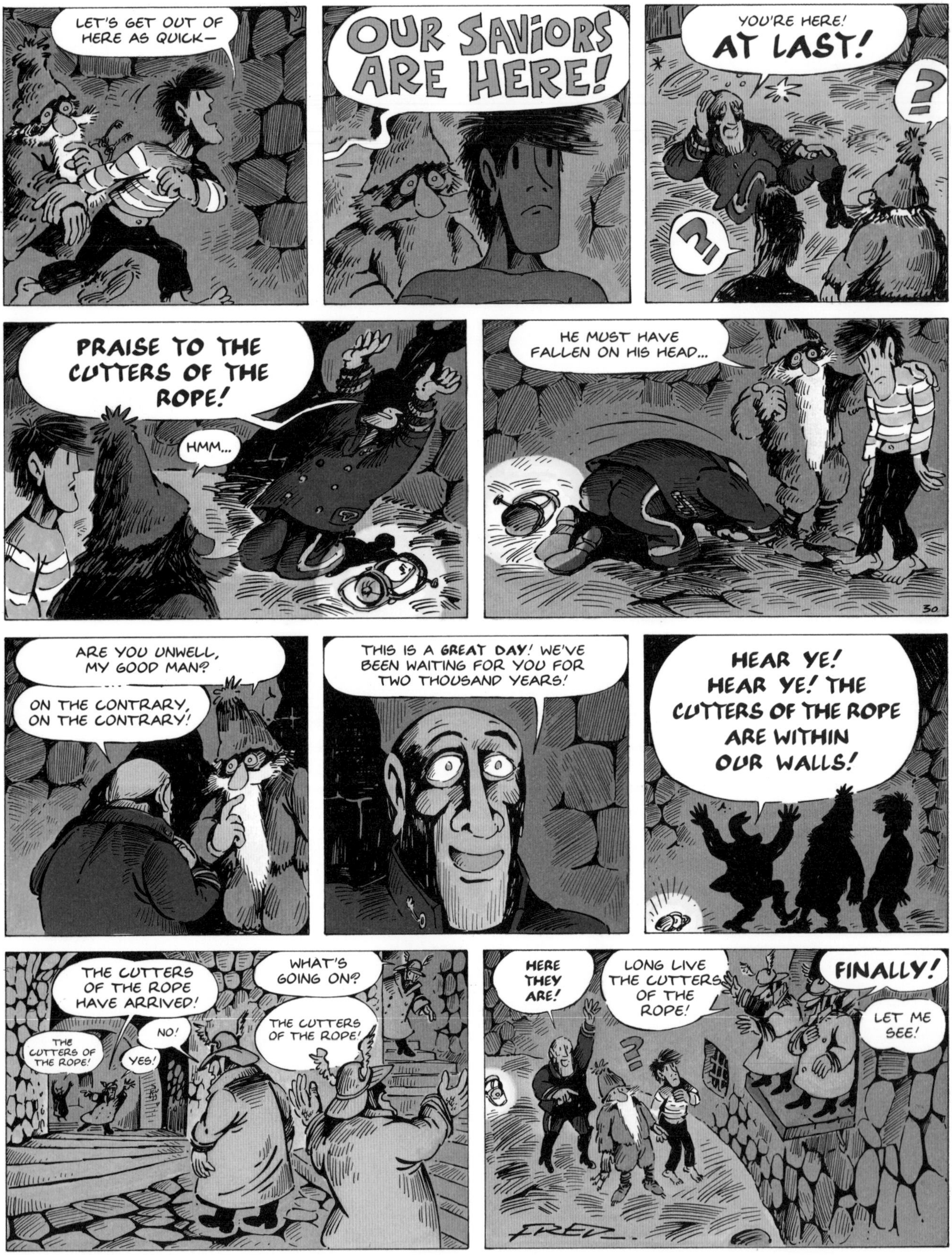

LET'S GET OUT OF HERE AS QUICK—
OUR SAVIORS ARE HERE!
YOU'RE HERE! AT LAST!
?
?!
PRAISE TO THE CUTTERS OF THE ROPE!
HMM...
HE MUST HAVE FALLEN ON HIS HEAD...
30.
ARE YOU UNWELL, MY GOOD MAN?
ON THE CONTRARY, ON THE CONTRARY!
THIS IS A GREAT DAY! WE'VE BEEN WAITING FOR YOU FOR TWO THOUSAND YEARS!
HEAR YE! HEAR YE! THE CUTTERS OF THE ROPE ARE WITHIN OUR WALLS!
THE CUTTERS OF THE ROPE HAVE ARRIVED!
WHAT'S GOING ON?
THE CUTTERS OF THE ROPE!
NO!
YES!
THE CUTTERS OF THE ROPE!
HERE THEY ARE!
LONG LIVE THE CUTTERS OF THE ROPE!
?
FINALLY!
LET ME SEE!
FRED

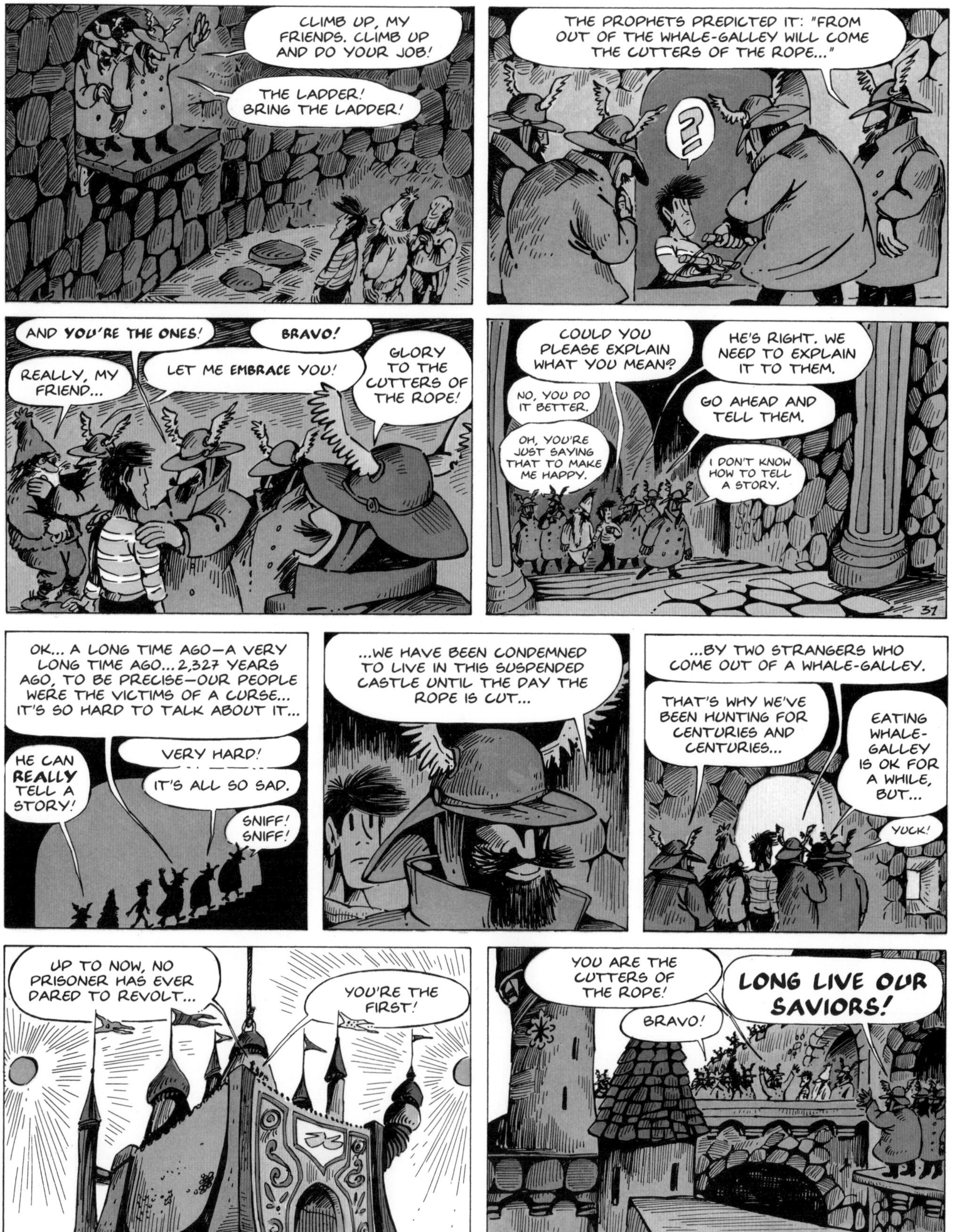
CLIMB UP, MY FRIENDS. CLIMB UP AND DO YOUR JOB!
THE LADDER! BRING THE LADDER!
THE PROPHETS PREDICTED IT: "FROM OUT OF THE WHALE-GALLEY WILL COME THE CUTTERS OF THE ROPE..."
?
AND YOU'RE THE ONES!
BRAVO!
REALLY, MY FRIEND...
LET ME EMBRACE YOU!
GLORY TO THE CUTTERS OF THE ROPE!
COULD YOU PLEASE EXPLAIN WHAT YOU MEAN?
HE'S RIGHT. WE NEED TO EXPLAIN IT TO THEM.
NO, YOU DO IT BETTER.
GO AHEAD AND TELL THEM.
OH, YOU'RE JUST SAYING THAT TO MAKE ME HAPPY.
I DON'T KNOW HOW TO TELL A STORY.
31
OK... A LONG TIME AGO—A VERY LONG TIME AGO... 2,327 YEARS AGO, TO BE PRECISE—OUR PEOPLE WERE THE VICTIMS OF A CURSE... IT'S SO HARD TO TALK ABOUT IT...
HE CAN REALLY TELL A STORY!
VERY HARD!
IT'S ALL SO SAD.
SNIFF! SNIFF!
...WE HAVE BEEN CONDEMNED TO LIVE IN THIS SUSPENDED CASTLE UNTIL THE DAY THE ROPE IS CUT...
...BY TWO STRANGERS WHO COME OUT OF A WHALE-GALLEY.
THAT'S WHY WE'VE BEEN HUNTING FOR CENTURIES AND CENTURIES...
EATING WHALE-GALLEY IS OK FOR A WHILE, BUT...
YUCK!
UP TO NOW, NO PRISONER HAS EVER DARED TO REVOLT...
YOU'RE THE FIRST!
YOU ARE THE CUTTERS OF THE ROPE!
LONG LIVE OUR SAVIORS!
BRAVO!

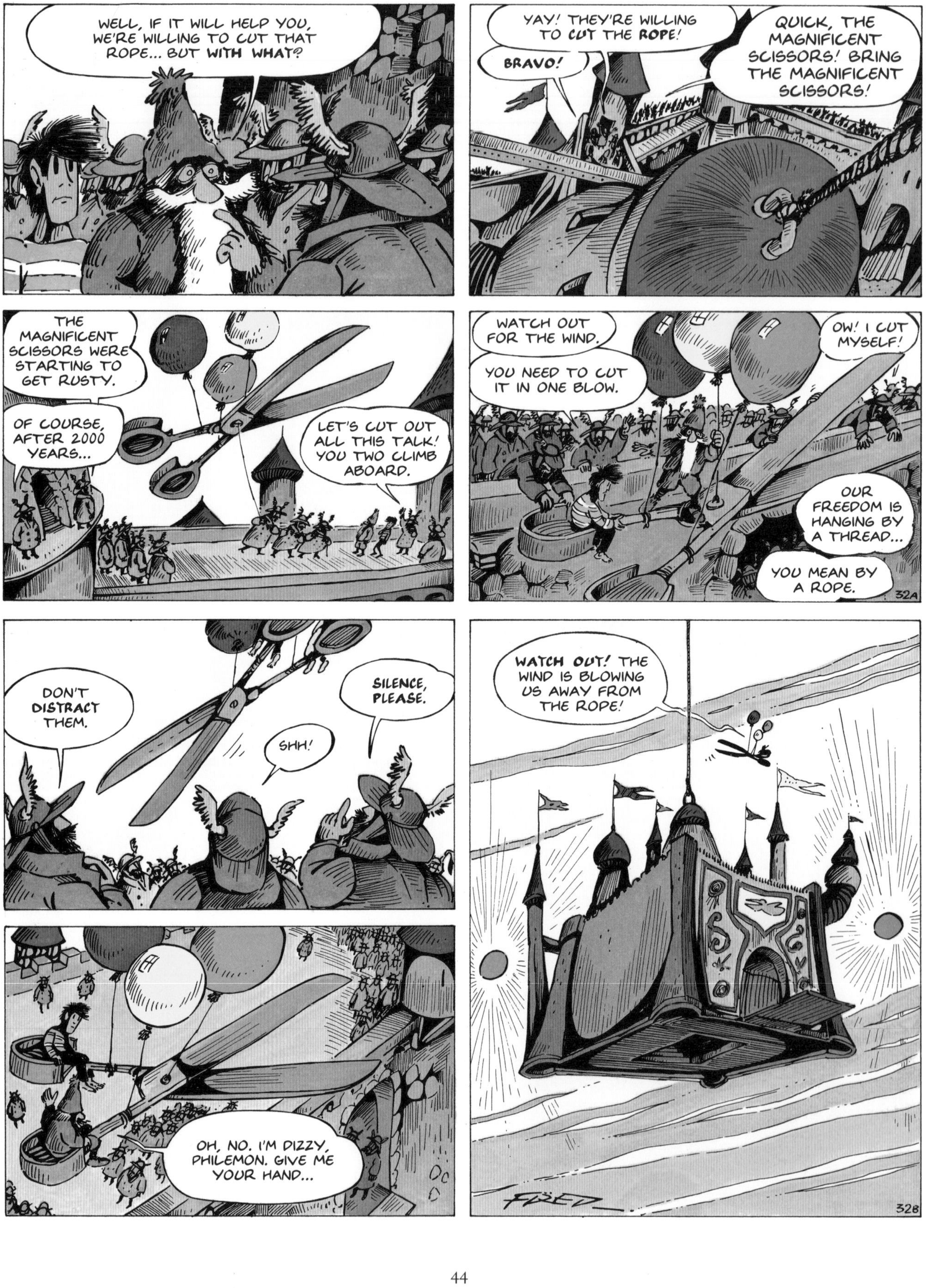
WELL, IF IT WILL HELP YOU, WE'RE WILLING TO CUT THAT ROPE... BUT WITH WHAT?
YAY! THEY'RE WILLING TO CUT THE ROPE!
BRAVO!
QUICK, THE MAGNIFICENT SCISSORS! BRING THE MAGNIFICENT SCISSORS!
THE MAGNIFICENT SCISSORS WERE STARTING TO GET RUSTY.
OF COURSE, AFTER 2000 YEARS...
LET'S CUT OUT ALL THIS TALK! YOU TWO CLIMB ABOARD.
WATCH OUT FOR THE WIND.
YOU NEED TO CUT IT IN ONE BLOW.
OW! I CUT MYSELF!
OUR FREEDOM IS HANGING BY A THREAD...
YOU MEAN BY A ROPE.
32A
DON'T DISTRACT THEM.
SHH!
SILENCE, PLEASE.
OH, NO. I'M DIZZY, PHILEMON. GIVE ME YOUR HAND...
WATCH OUT! THE WIND IS BLOWING US AWAY FROM THE ROPE!
FRED
32B

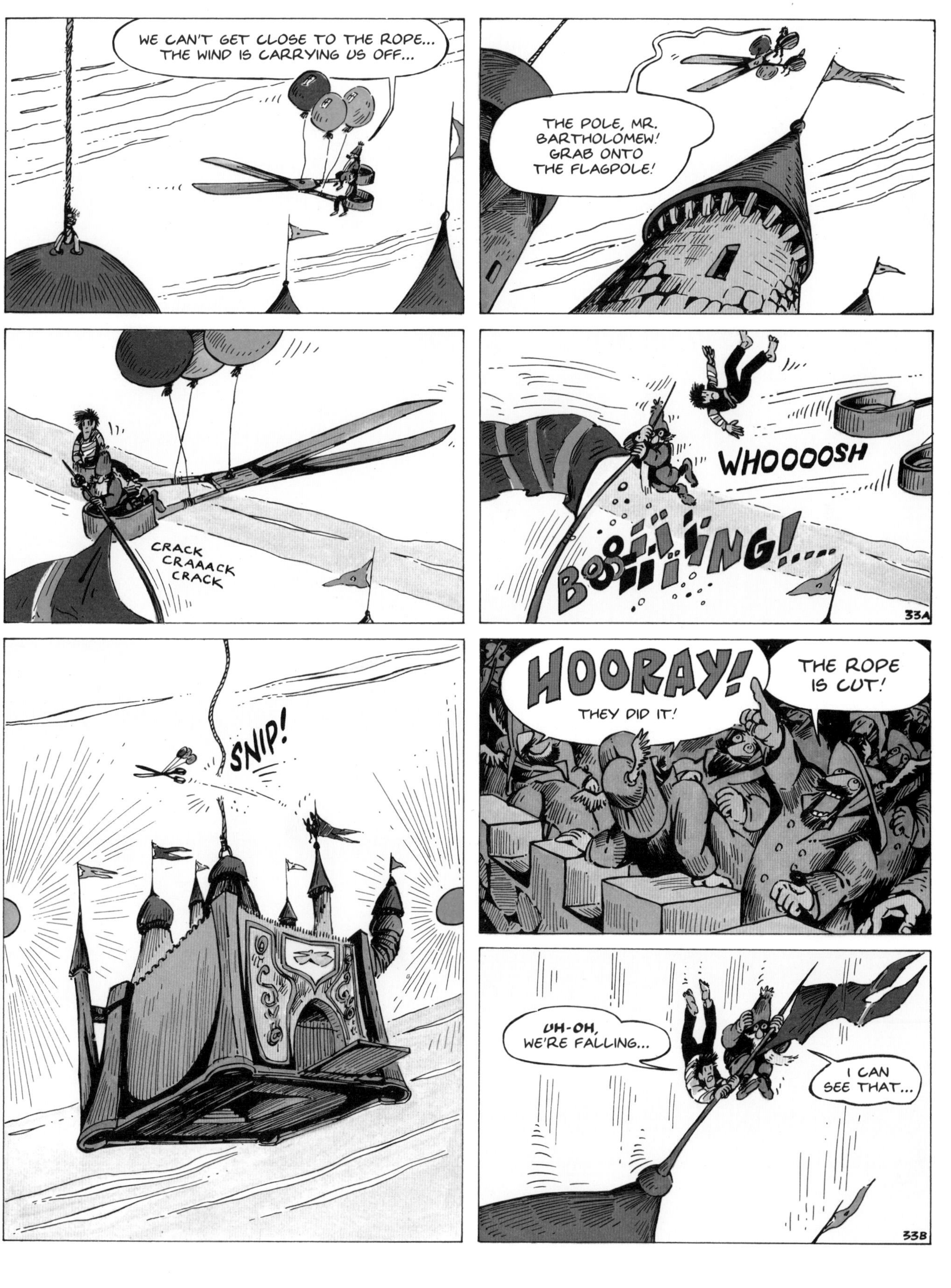
WE CAN'T GET CLOSE TO THE ROPE... THE WIND IS CARRYING US OFF...
THE POLE, MR. BARTHOLOMEW! GRAB ONTO THE FLAGPOLE!
CRACK CRAAACK CRACK
WHOOOOSH
BOOIIIING!....
33A
SNIP!
HOORAY!
THEY DID IT!
THE ROPE IS CUT!
UH-OH, WE'RE FALLING...
I CAN SEE THAT...
33B

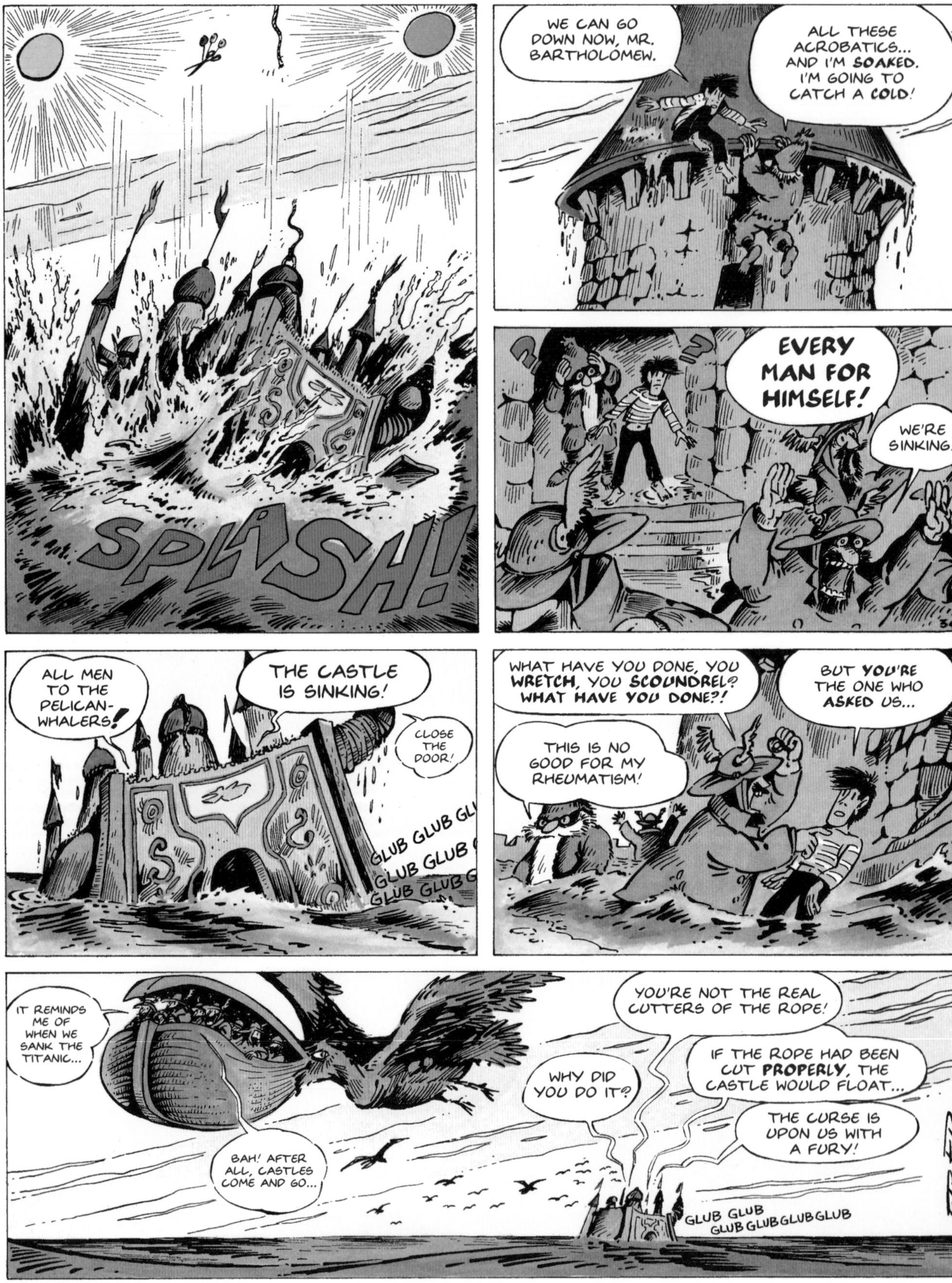
SPLASH!
WE CAN GO DOWN NOW, MR. BARTHOLOMEW.
ALL THESE ACROBATICS... AND I'M SOAKED. I'M GOING TO CATCH A COLD!
EVERY MAN FOR HIMSELF!
WE'RE SINKING!
ALL MEN TO THE PELICAN-WHALERS!
THE CASTLE IS SINKING!
CLOSE THE DOOR!
GLUB GLUB GLUB GLUB GLUB GLUB GLUB
WHAT HAVE YOU DONE, YOU WRETCH, YOU SCOUNDREL? WHAT HAVE YOU DONE?!
BUT YOU'RE THE ONE WHO ASKED US...
THIS IS NO GOOD FOR MY RHEUMATISM!
IT REMINDS ME OF WHEN WE SANK THE TITANIC...
BAH! AFTER ALL, CASTLES COME AND GO...
WHY DID YOU DO IT?
YOU'RE NOT THE REAL CUTTERS OF THE ROPE!
IF THE ROPE HAD BEEN CUT PROPERLY, THE CASTLE WOULD FLOAT...
THE CURSE IS UPON US WITH A FURY!
GLUB GLUB GLUB GLUB GLUB GLUB
FRED

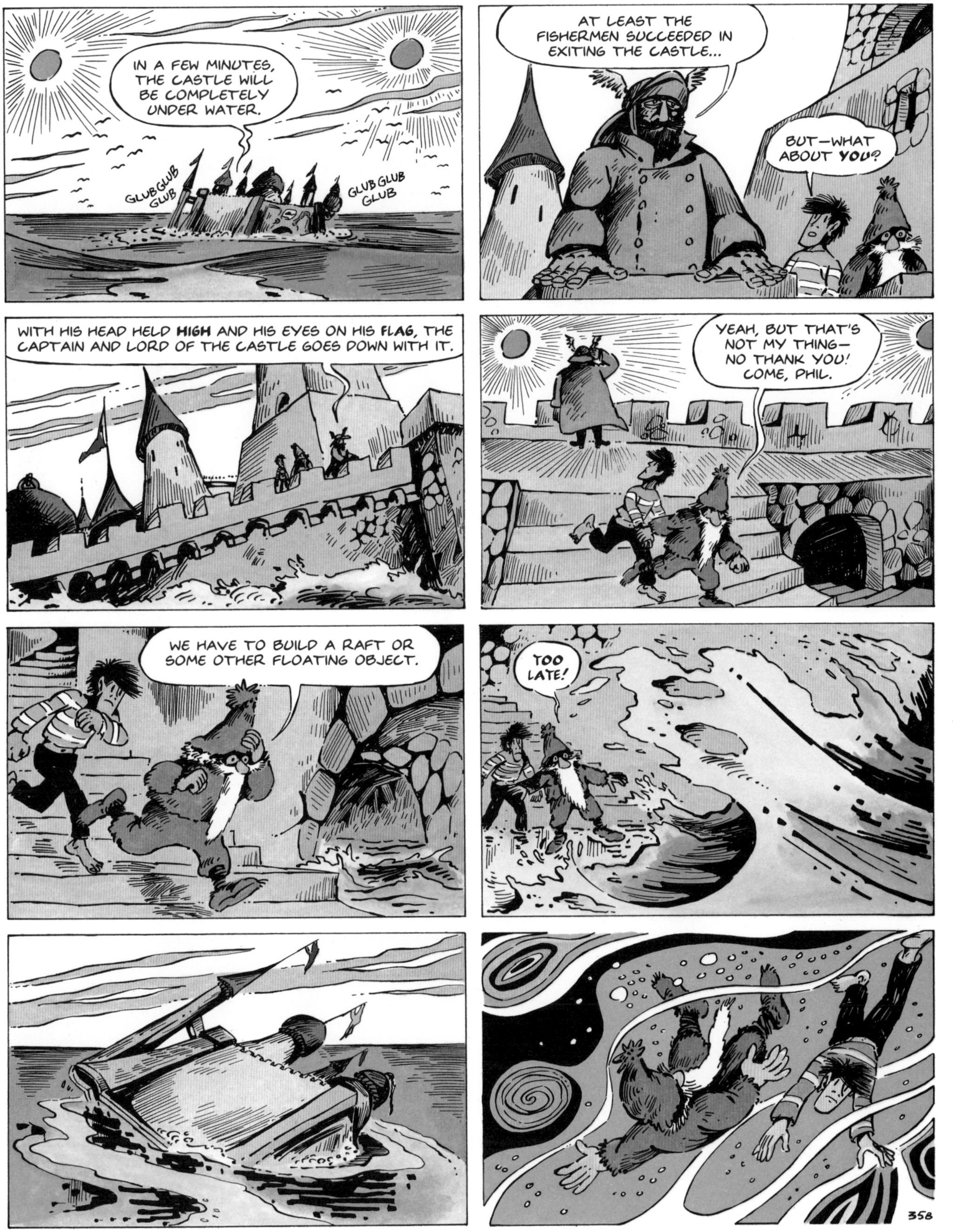
IN A FEW MINUTES, THE CASTLE WILL BE COMPLETELY UNDER WATER.
GLUB GLUB GLUB
GLUB GLUB GLUB
AT LEAST THE FISHERMEN SUCCEEDED IN EXITING THE CASTLE...
BUT—WHAT ABOUT YOU?
WITH HIS HEAD HELD HIGH AND HIS EYES ON HIS FLAG, THE CAPTAIN AND LORD OF THE CASTLE GOES DOWN WITH IT.
YEAH, BUT THAT'S NOT MY THING— NO THANK YOU! COME, PHIL.
WE HAVE TO BUILD A RAFT OR SOME OTHER FLOATING OBJECT.
TOO LATE!
358

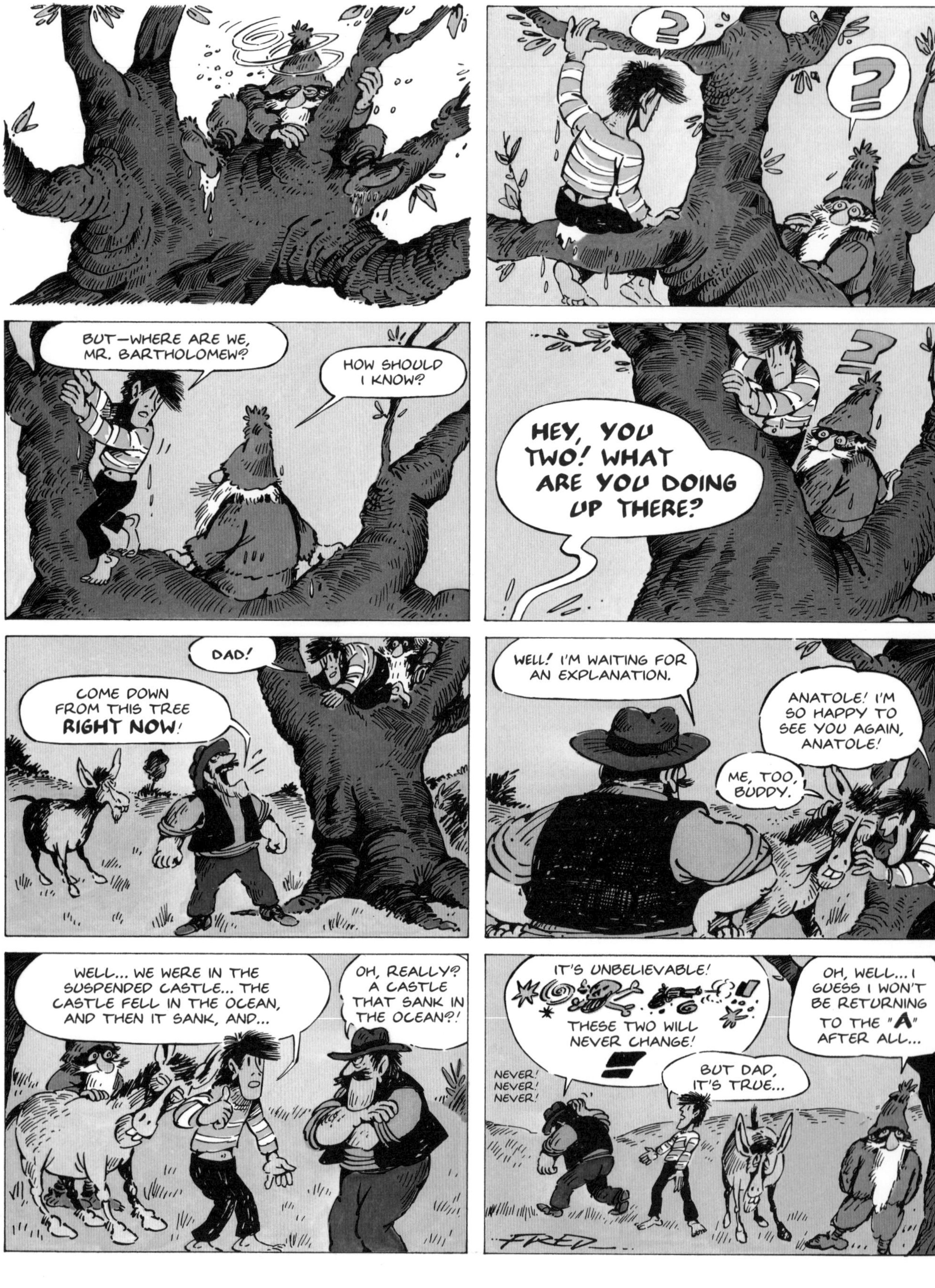

BUT—WHERE ARE WE, MR. BARTHOLOMEW?
HOW SHOULD I KNOW?
HEY, YOU TWO! WHAT ARE YOU DOING UP THERE?
36
DAD!
COME DOWN FROM THIS TREE **RIGHT NOW**!
WELL! I'M WAITING FOR AN EXPLANATION.
ANATOLE! I'M SO HAPPY TO SEE YOU AGAIN, ANATOLE!
ME, TOO, BUDDY.
WELL... WE WERE IN THE SUSPENDED CASTLE... THE CASTLE FELL IN THE OCEAN, AND THEN IT SANK, AND...
OH, REALLY? A CASTLE THAT SANK IN THE OCEAN?!
IT'S UNBELIEVABLE!
THESE TWO WILL NEVER CHANGE!
NEVER! NEVER! NEVER!
BUT DAD, IT'S TRUE...
OH, WELL... I GUESS I WON'T BE RETURNING TO THE "A" AFTER ALL...
FRED

I'M PLAYING A SMALLER AND SMALLER ROLE IN EACH EPISODE.

FRED.

Down the well, in a world of utter fantasy...

Frédéric Othon Aristidès (1931-2013), known as Fred, was of France's most influential and revered cartoonists. In the sixties, he co-founded *Hara-Kiri*, the leading satirical publication of the May '68 movement and the predecessor of *Charlie Hebdo*. *Philémon*, his story for young readers and his most celebrated creation, was first published in *Pilote* in 1965 by René Goscinny, the author of *Astérix*. Millions of French people have grown up with it, and it has inspired many of today's most talented cartoonists.

Fred was born in Paris to a Greek immigrant family. The young Fred grew up hearing nightly stories from his mother, inspired by Greek mythology, French fairy tales, and the British literature she herself had grown up with. He kept the habit all his life: every night as he drifted to sleep, he gave himself a few unrelated words (such as whale, owl, or galley ship) and built a story around it. While there's no knowing where exactly he found his inspiration, he said he often got his best ideas while taking a bath. In the following pages, we reference some of the sources of his fertile imagination.

Whaling

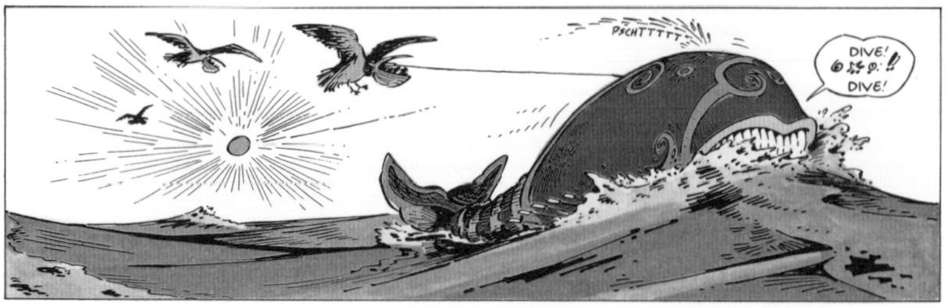
PSCHTTTTTT
DIVE!
DIVE!

The hunting of whales has existed for thousands of years. Whales, which are mammals (not fish), have been hunted for their meat and their oil, which was used to light lamps before the discovery of electricity. People also used to harvest whale's baleen (also referred to as "whalebone") to make corset boning, collar stiffeners, parasol ribs, and paper-folders. Whales were usually killed by harpoons, which were shot or thrown from boats. In 1851, Herman Melville, an American author who had been a sailor, published his masterpiece, *Moby Dick*, about a captain's quest to kill a great white whale. By the late 1930s, more than fifty thousand whales were killed each year. There is much debate today as to whether whales should still be hunted.

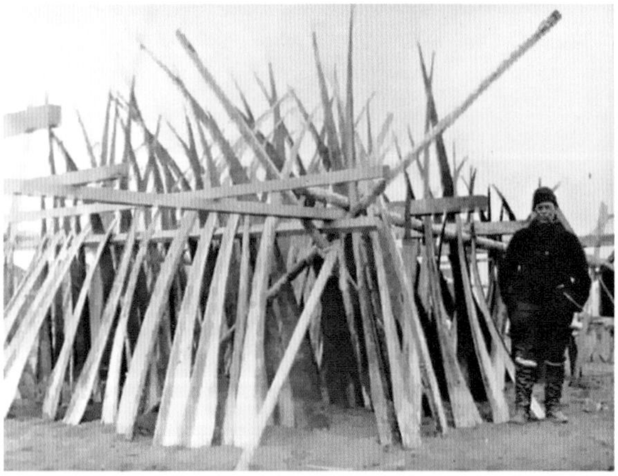

"Pieces of cleaned baleen," ca. 1900. Alaska State Library, Rev. Samuel Spriggs Photograph Collection.

A whaler with a collection of baleen.

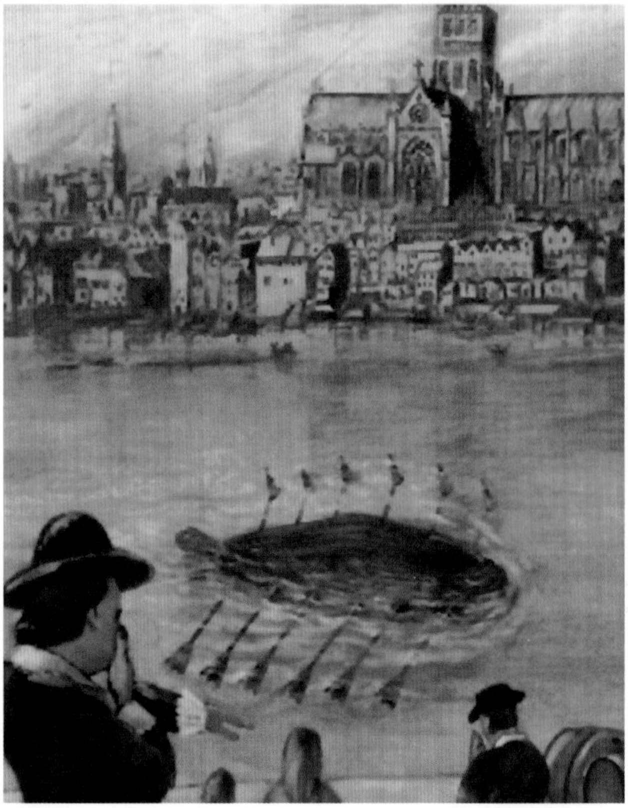

G. H. Tweedale, "The Drebbel," ca. 1970. Royal Submarine Museum.

One of the first submersible boats, known as The Drebbel, *was built by Cornelius Drebbel in 1620. It looked like a whale and was powered by oars.*

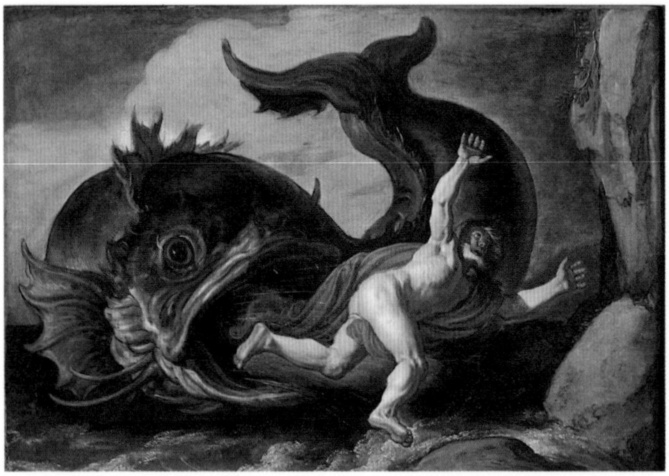

Pieter Lastman, "Jonah and the Whale," 1621.

Jonah and the Whale

Jonah is a prophet who appears in the Old Testament of the Bible and in several sections of the Qur'an. According to religious texts, Jonah disobeyed God's command to alert the people of Nineveh, capital of Assyria, that they were to be destroyed because of their wickedness. Jonah fled by ship but was thrown overboard by the sailors in a storm. He was swallowed by a whale or a giant fish (depending on the translation) and spent three days and nights inside it before being spat out.

Galleys

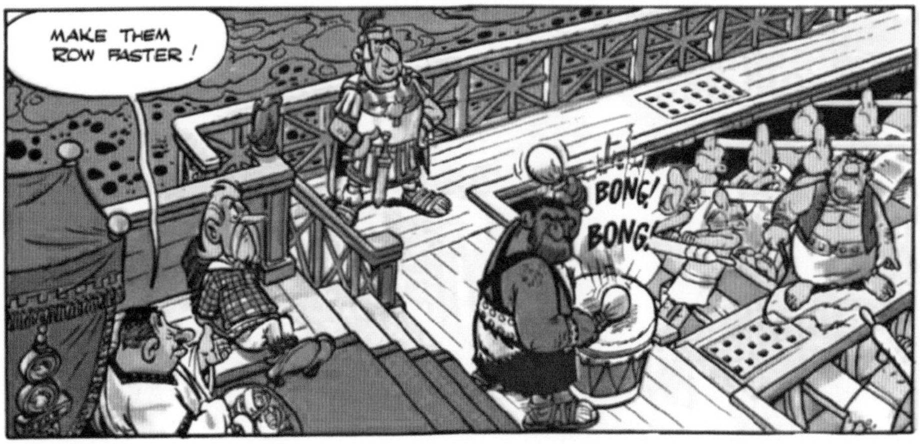
MAKE THEM ROW FASTER!
BONG!
BONG!
Asterix the Gladiator © 1964 Goscinny & Uderzo

A galley in Asterix the Gladiator, *originally published in* Pilote, *the same magazine that published* Philemon.

Galleys are wooden ships that are propelled by rowers. They were used for trade and warfare in the Mediterranean Sea as long as three thousand years ago. Some had one row of rowers (monoremes), some had two (biremes), and some had three (triremes). Galleys often had drummers to help rowers keep a steady pace. Rowers allowed the ships to move against the current or even when there was no wind. Of course, rowers took up a great deal of space, and a lot of food had to be kept on board to feed them. This made them impractical for long, ocean-going voyages. It was not unusual to sentence criminals to galley service, and "galley slaves" were sometimes even enlisted from captives and prisoners of war. Galleys were still used for warfare, trade, and piracy as late as the nineteenth century.

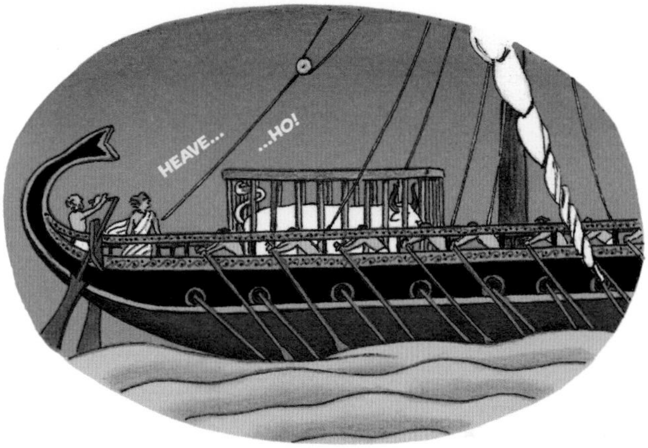
HEAVE...
...HO!

A Cretan galley from Theseus and the Minotaur *by Yvan Pommaux, another TOON Graphic.*

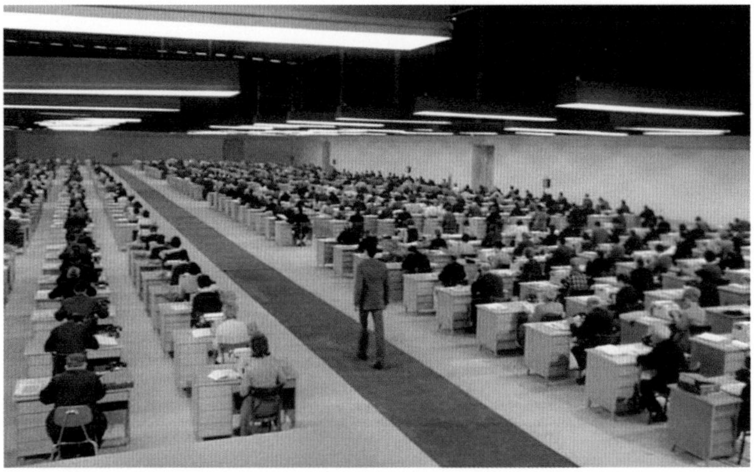

A still from Orson Welles's 1962 film adaptation of The Trial.

The Trial

In *The Trial* by Franz Kafka, a German-speaking Czech author, a man is arrested and put on trial for a crime that is never revealed to him or the reader. This is similar to the way Philemon and Bartholomew are put to work in the whale-galley but have no idea where they are going.

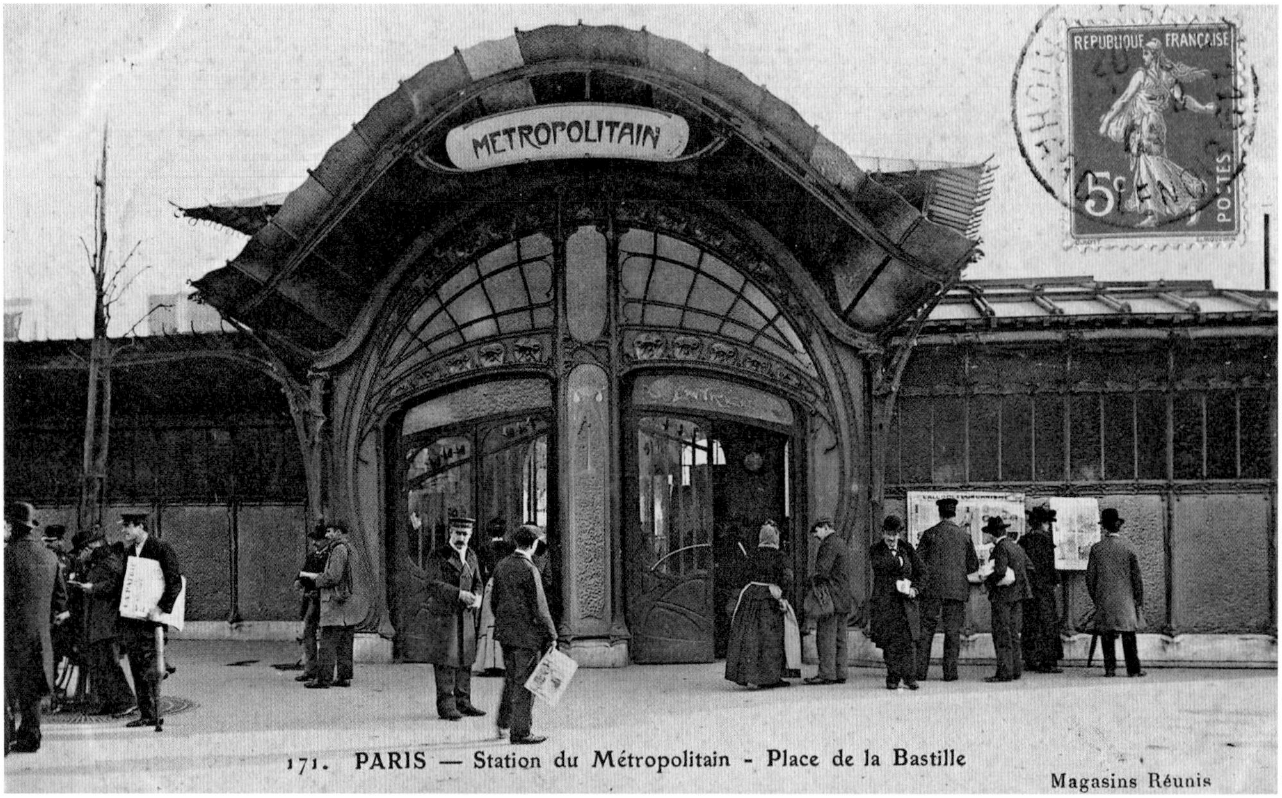
METROPOLITAIN
REPUBLIQUE FRANÇAISE
5c
POSTES
171. PARIS — Station du Métropolitain - Place de la Bastille
Magasins Réunis

Postcard of Hector Guimard's Bastille Station, ca. 1900.

The Paris Métro

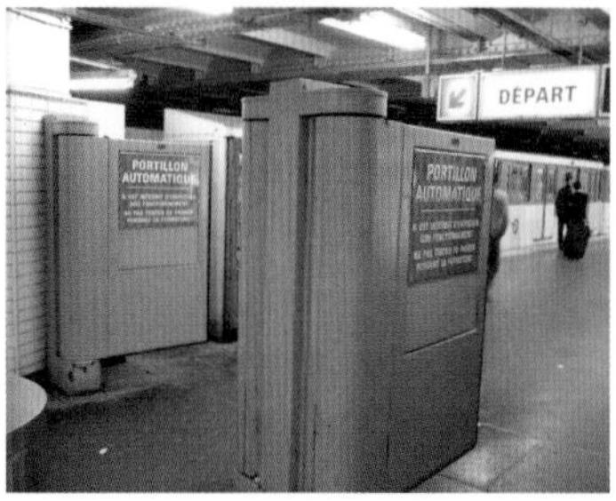
DEPART
PORTILLON AUTOMATIQUE
PORTILLON AUTOMATIQUE

The first line of the Paris subway, or Métropolitain, opened in 1900, during the World's Fair. Many of the entrances still have the flowery Art Nouveau ironwork designed by the architect Hector Guimard. There are now sixteen lines with 303 stations, including the largest one in the world, *Châtelet-Les Halles,* and the Métro carries more than four million passengers a day. Métro stations used to have heavy gates called *portillons*–pictured above and in this book–to keep people from getting hurt as they rushed to trains that were about to close their doors and zoom off. Since 2000, several lines have become entirely automated and driverless. On those lines, the train enters the station in a glass tube whose doors line up to those of the cars and open when the train is in place. One can only imagine what Fred would have made of that design if he had been writing today.

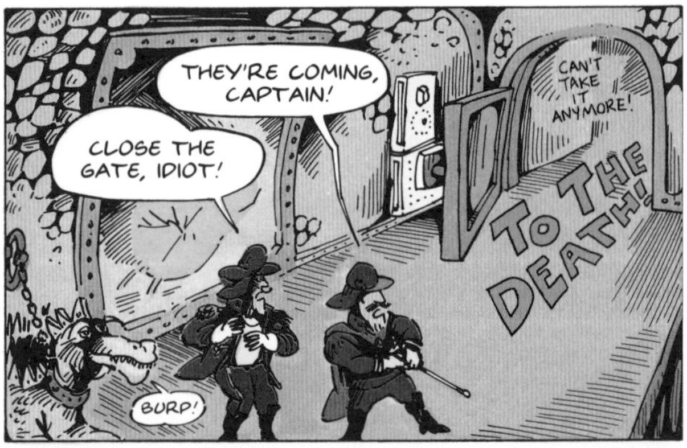
THEY'RE COMING, CAPTAIN!
CLOSE THE GATE, IDIOT!
CAN'T TAKE IT ANYMORE!
TO THE DEATH!
BURP!

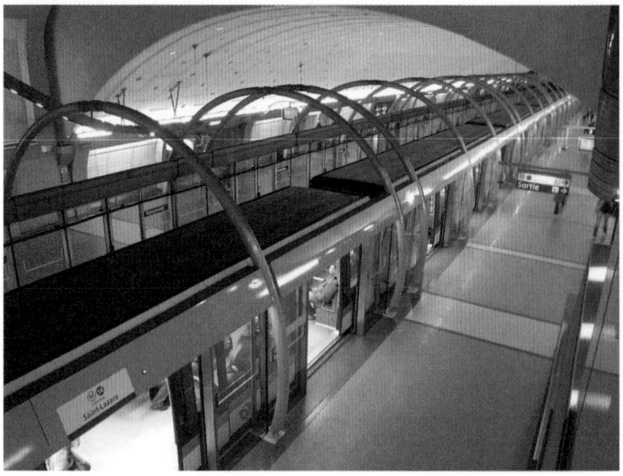

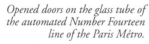

Opened doors on the glass tube of the automated Number Fourteen line of the Paris Métro.

Photo by Pline, 2006, licensed under Creative Commons.

Lighthouses

The earliest lighthouses were constructed in ancient times, before the third century BCE. Although they were initially lit by fires (instead of lamps), the purpose was the same: to guide ships in a dark ocean. Today, the use of lighthouses has declined due to replacement by modern electronic navigational systems. Fred's owl-lighthouse takes the idea of "guiding sailors across the ocean" more literally, however, allowing seafarers to walk on the beams of light themselves!

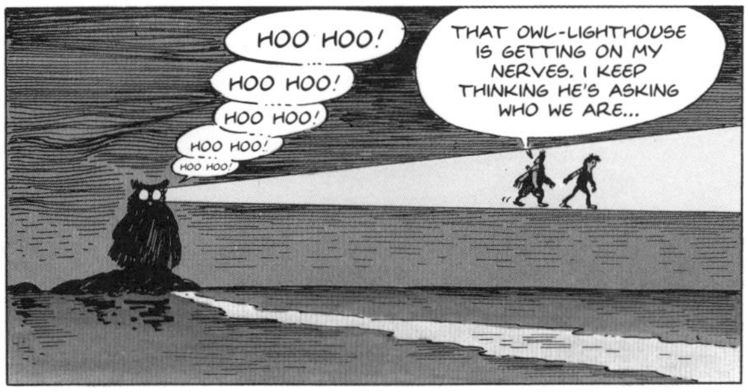
HOO HOO!
HOO HOO!
HOO HOO!
HOO HOO!
HOO HOO!
THAT OWL-LIGHTHOUSE IS GETTING ON MY NERVES. I KEEP THINKING HE'S ASKING WHO WE ARE...

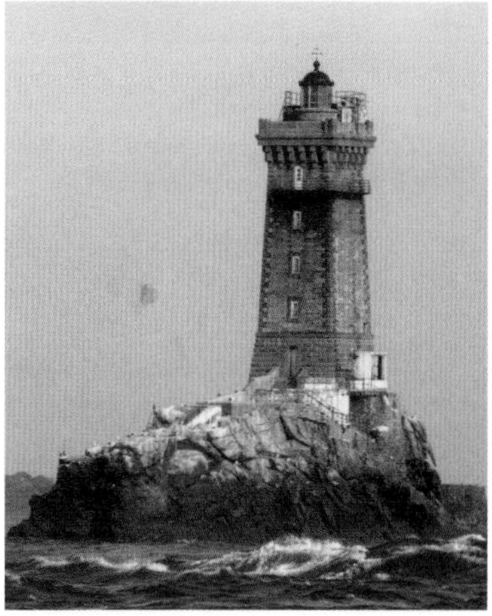

Postcard of La Vieille Lighthouse, ca. 2000.

The Old Lady Lighthouse in Brittany, France, built in 1887, housed a keeper until it was automated in 1995.

Castles in the Air

Suspended, flying, or floating castles (or cities) are now a common theme in science fiction and fantasy. Floating islands appear in Homer's *Odyssey* and in Jonathan Swift's 1726 satirical novel, *Gulliver's Travels*, in which the hero visits a floating island city called Laputa. Laputa appears in the Japanese title of Hayao Miyazaki's 1986 animated film *The Castle in the Sky*. Fred's book precedes Miyazaki's work and may have provided inspiration, just as Fred himself may have seen *The Castle of the Pyrenees*, a 1959 painting by Belgian Surrealist René Magritte, in which a castle on a boulder defies gravity over a stormy ocean.

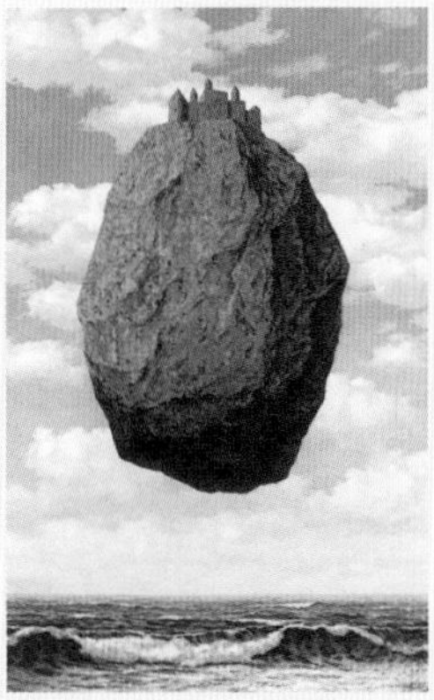

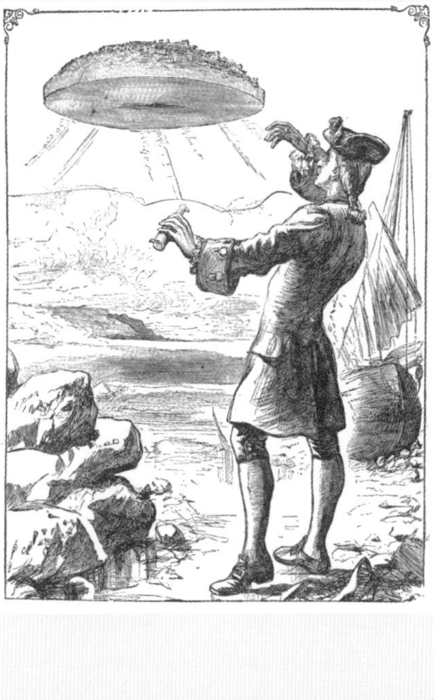

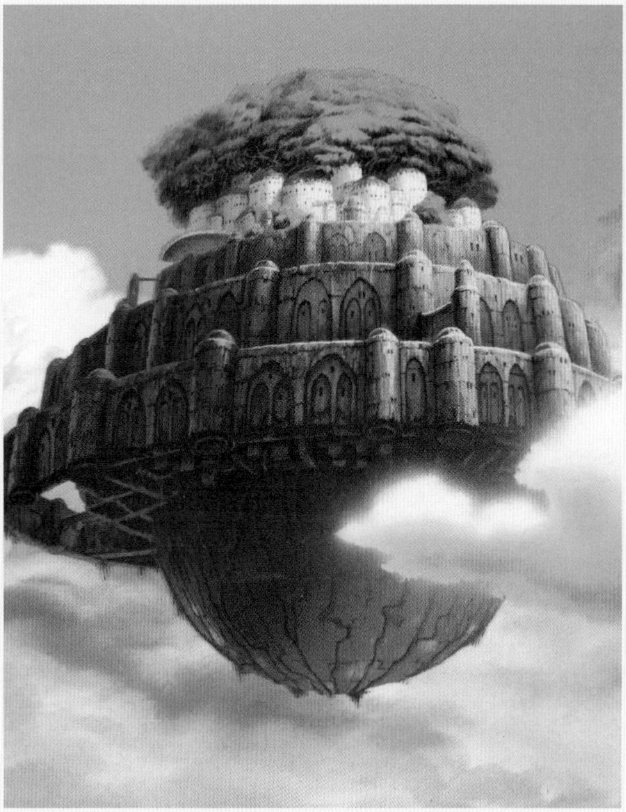

Top left: The Castle of the Pyrenees, *1959, a painting by Belgian Surrealist painter René Magritte.* Above: *Publicity still from the film* Laputa: The Castle in the Sky *by Hayao Miyazaki, 1986.* Left: *J.J. Grandville, Illustration of Laputa from* Gulliver's Travels, *1838.*

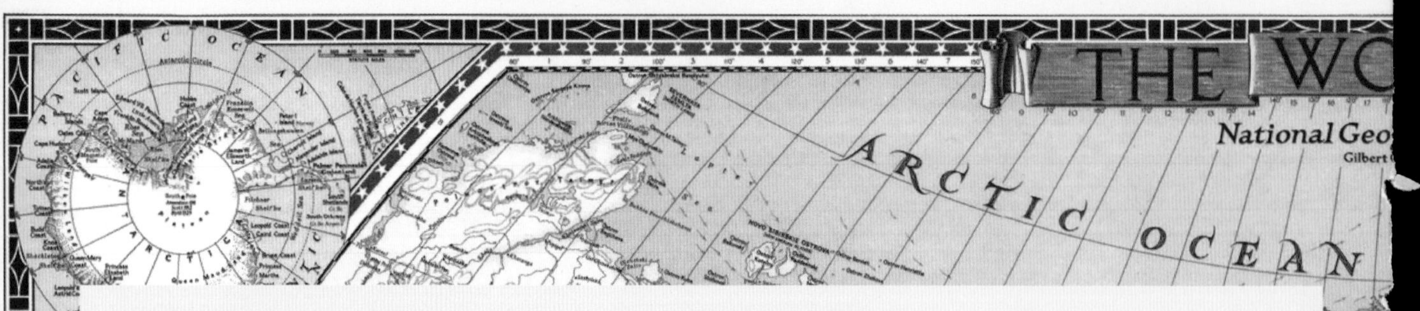
THE WO
National Geo
ARCTIC OCEAN

Tips for Parents, Teachers, and Librarians:

TOON GRAPHICS FOR VISUAL READERS

TOON Graphics are comics and visual narratives that bring the text to life in a way that captures young readers' imaginations and makes them want to read on—and read more. When the authors are also artists, they can convey their creative vision with pictures as well as words. They can enhance the overarching theme and present important details that are absorbed by the reader along with the text. Young readers also develop their aesthetic sense when they experience the relationship of text to picture in all its communicative power.

Reading TOON Graphics is a pleasure for all. Beginners and seasoned readers alike will sharpen both their literal and inferential reading skills.

Let the pictures tell the story

The very economy of comic books necessitates the use of a reader's imaginative powers. In comics, the images often imply rather than tell outright. Readers must learn to make connections between events to complete the narrative, helping them build their ability to visualize and to make "mental maps."

A comic book also gives readers a great deal of visual context that can be used to investigate the thinking behind the characters' choices.

Pay attention to the artist's choices

Look carefully at the artwork: it offers a subtext that at first is sensed only on a subliminal level by the reader and encourages rereading. It creates a sense of continuity for the action, and it can tell you about the art, architecture, and clothing of a specific time period. It may present the atmosphere, landscape, and flora and fauna of another time or of another part of the world. TOON Graphics can also present multiple points of view and simultaneous events in a manner not permitted by linear written narration. Facial expressions and body language reveal subtle aspects of characters' personalities beyond what can be expressed by words.

Read and reread!

Readers can compare comic book artists' styles and evaluate how different authors get their point across in different ways. In investigating the author's choices, a young reader begins to gain a sense of how all literary and art forms can be used to convey the author's central ideas.

The world of TOON Graphics and of comic book art is rich and varied. Making meaning out of reading with the aid of visuals may be the best way to become a lifelong reader, one who knows how to read for pleasure and for information—a reader who *loves* to read.

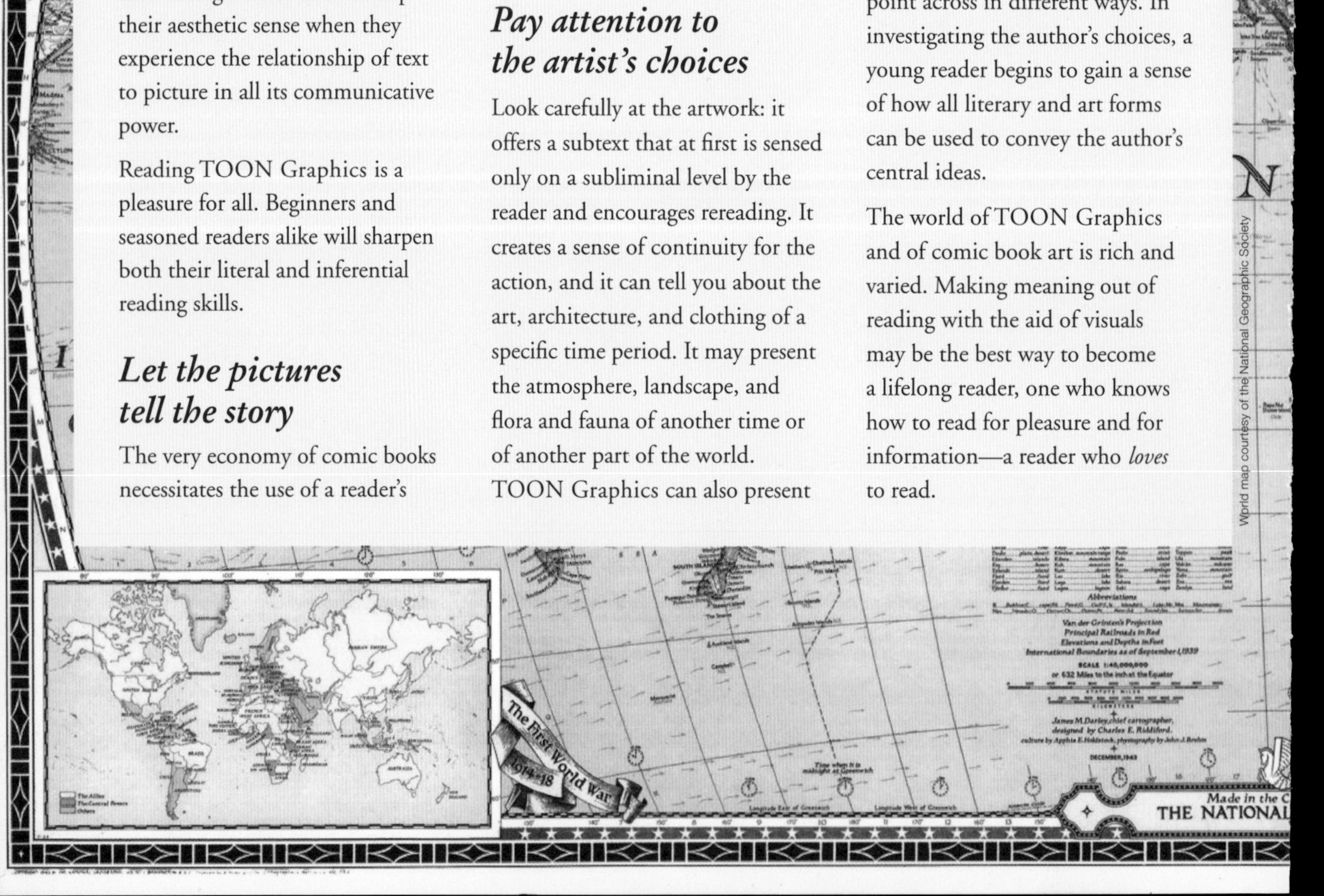
The First World War 1914–18
Made in the C
THE NATIONAL